"A *Pilgrim's Progress* for the
Chuck Black has achieved in
of the whole Bible told in a medieval format of noble
knights and scathing sword fights, quests and dragons,
betrayal and final victory by the true Prince over the Dark
Knight."

—DAVE JACKSON
author of the *Trailblazer* novels

"Take up the sword handed to you and boldly carry it
through the pages of Chuck Black's Kingdom Series. You'll
be held captive by a creative journey through a distant
world that leads to God's Word…and a kingdom like no
other."

—TIM WESEMANN
author of *Swashbuckling Faith:*
Exploring for Treasure with Pirates of the Caribbean

THE KINGDOM SERIES

BOOK 3

KINGDOM'S EDGE

CHUCK BLACK

MULTNOMAH

KINGDOM'S EDGE

© 1999, 2006 by Chuck Black
Published in association with The Steve Laube Agency, LLC,
5501 North Seventh Avenue #502, Phoenix, AZ 85013

International Standard Book Number: 978-1-59052-681-1

Interior design and typeset by Katherine Lloyd, The DESK
Interior illustration by Marcella Johnson
"Deliverance" music © 2002 by Emily Elizabeth Black;
lyrics © 2002 by Chuck Black

Unless otherwise indicated, Scripture quotations are from:
The Holy Bible, New King James Version
© 1984 by Thomas Nelson, Inc.

Published in the United States by Multnomah, an imprint of the Crown Publishing Group, a division of Penguin Random House LLC,
New York.

MULTNOMAH® and its mountain colophon are registered trademarks of Penguin Random House LLC.

Printed in the United States of America

Library of Congress Cataloging-in-Publication Data
Black, Chuck.
 Kingdom's edge / Chuck Black.
   p. cm. -- (The kingdom series ; bk. 3)
 ISBN 1-59052-681-3
 I. Title.
 PS3602.L264K56 2006
 813'.6--dc22

                                                    2006005492

20 — 19

To my devoted wife and editor, Andrea,
and to my children,
Brittney, Reese, Ian, Emily, Abigail, and Keenan.

CONTENTS

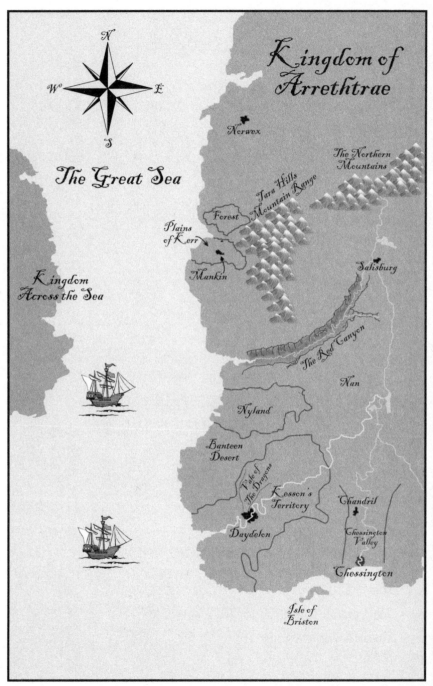

© Chuck Black

SOMETHING EVIL COMES OUR WAY

 My heart is beating rapidly. My eyes are focused. I can see the dust rising in the distance. Something massive and evil is coming our way.

As I scan the horizon from left to right, my eyes come to rest on the line of gallant knights beside me that stretches as far as the eye can see. They are men of courage and valor. Yes, I am in that noble line as well. My steed's muscles twitch with power in anticipation of the coming battle. My armor shines, and the helmet fits my brow comfortably. My sword, polished and sharp, gleams in the sunlight. I have worked my sword for months in preparation for this very moment.

I am an unlikely knight. Cedric is my name. I come from the city of Chessington, in the kingdom of Arrethtrae.

A few short years ago you would not have believed that I would be telling you this tale of battles, knights, and swords. Time has gone quickly. I remember when I was but a peasant...

CHAPTER ONE

A STRANGER
IN OUR MIDST

 "Cedric, if you don't hurry, we'll miss the procession," William called.

William was a dreamer. Unfortunately, these were times when not even dreamers could hope for a brighter tomorrow. Although his heart was tender, his features were sharp, giving the false impression that he was a hard man. William was strong and knew where he wanted to be, but he was not sure how to get there. His hair was dark and matched his brown eyes. Taller than average, he was a handsome man. I had known him since I was a boy. He was my friend.

"William, you know I've got to check on Leinad first," I said. "Besides, what is so grand about seeing not-so-noble Noble Knights pass by when my stomach howls in hunger?"

"If only we were one of them, we wouldn't *be* hungry," William said as we approached an old cottage that matched the age of its lone occupant.

"You're dreaming again, William. We were not born of noble blood and will therefore never become Noble Knights. Get that foolish notion out of your head!"

Leinad lived just outside Chessington near a small stream that lazily wound its way toward the sea to the south. He was a strange fellow. I had come to know him when I was a young lad. People tend to avoid what they cannot understand or what makes them uncomfortable, and this was the case with Leinad.

Although most people avoided him, I was drawn to him and his stories—stories that seemed too strange to be true and too original to be fabricated. If even a small portion of the tales were true, then Chessington was ignorant of a very gallant man. If the tales were indeed made-up, then Leinad was just as everyone thought him to be: insane. Either way, I had a tender spot in my heart for him, especially since he was now too old to properly care for himself.

"Good day, Sir Leinad!" I raised my voice in greeting as we approached his door. Many of his stories portrayed him as a knight in service to the King. I half-jokingly addressed him as such, but I could never tell if I was humoring him or if he was humoring me by graciously accepting my flippant use of the title.

"Ah, dear Cedric," came the familiar warm voice. "Welcome to my palace. Please come in."

We stepped into his home to see Leinad seated at a small table near the south wall. His left hand was resting on the sill of the window he was staring through.

His silver hair and brows partnered with his bent frame

to paint a picture of a man near the end of life's journey. He attempted to rise and meet us, but I halted him as I placed my hand on his shoulder.

"It's all right, Leinad," I said. "I know you are already standing in your heart."

"It is good to see you, Cedric and William," Leinad said with sincerity. He smiled at us with his eyes.

"Hello, Leinad," William said. "How are you feeling today?"

Leinad took in a deep breath, and he turned again toward the window.

"They listened once before, but time has defeated the sincerity of truth," Leinad said, answering a question no one had asked.

William glanced my way with a raised eyebrow. I smiled.

"We brought some bread for you," I said, trying to break his distant trance. "I will try to bring some fruit on my next visit, but the city is pretty short on food these days."

Leinad turned to us and gazed into my eyes. "*Time* is short," he said. "The power of the King is near, and the Dark One is mounted. You must be ready…the people must be ready!"

We were used to Leinad's odd talk, but today he seemed overcome with his delusions.

"My mission is nearly complete," he said. "The Sword of the King sings in anticipation of the One who is worthy!"

"Yes," I said, "your sword has no equal in splendor or beauty, that is certain. You have done well in its keeping." I rested my hand on his shoulder. "Leinad, we must leave you now, but I will return in a few days to check on you. We can talk more then."

Leinad smiled. "Very well, Cedric. Thank you for the bread. The King will remember your kindness to me."

I bowed and smiled as I winked at William. "Good day then, Sir Leinad," I said as we turned toward the door.

Outside William took a deep breath and shook his head.

"Someday, William, you and I will be hallucinating fools too," I said as we quickened our pace to make the procession.

"I don't think you should humor the old man so much," William said.

"What harm can it do? Leinad is old, and if he wants to spend his final years believing in something more than we are living…then why not?"

"Yes, but I think you crossed the line with that bit about the sword," William said as we entered the city.

"The sword is real," I said. Soon I realized I was walking by myself. I turned around to see William standing still with a perplexed look on his face.

"What?"

"Yes," I said. "Leinad owns a sword that is more magnificent than any I've ever seen—even more beautiful than any of the swords owned by the Noble Knights."

"Where did he get such a sword?" he asked, still not quite believing me.

"His story is long and bizarre, William. In truth, I do not know how he came to own it. He keeps it wrapped in a cloth in that old wooden chest in the corner. I fear that someone would kill him for it if they knew it was there. That is why I have told no one about it."

William rejoined me, but his gait was slower now, and his thoughts appeared to be deep.

"You're sure about this sword, Cedric?" he asked.

"It's been years, but I've seen it myself. It nearly glows in its splendor. Why someone would give a sword like that to Leinad is a mystery indeed."

At the city's main thoroughfare, we pushed our way to the front of the crowd. Beside us a woman with two small children waited, hoping for a scrap of food the Noble Knights might throw her way. The children's faces were as dirty as their clothes. Poverty overwhelmed the people.

The sound of hooves on cobblestone announced the knights' approach.

"Their horses prance and snort to match the arrogance of their riders," I said in low tones to William.

"Enough, Cedric. After all, these Noble Knights are the chosen, are they not?"

"The King has been gone so long that I wonder if He even remembers this dreadful land."

A poor old peasant woman was begging from one of the knights as he passed. "Please, good sir, a bit o' food for a hungry old woman?"

He laughed as he threw a half-eaten apple her way. "Don't eat it all at once," he sneered.

The old woman picked up the dirt-covered apple and ate it as though it was her last meal. Maybe it would be.

The Noble Knights often passed through the streets handing out tidbits of food to show their goodwill toward the people. I believed they did it to inflate their egos; they loved their position over the people. But they had been chosen by the King to defend our land, and from all I had heard of the King, He was just and fair. Somehow, since He'd left for another country, the welfare of the kingdom had continually declined.

"Here, old man, have a feast today."

One of the knights threw a loaf of bread to a bent old man just in front of me. I prepared for my opportunity, fully expecting the feeble old man to miss. I saw his hand reach up for the hurled loaf. The gnarled fingers I expected to see were not gnarled at all. The hand was quick and strong. He snatched the loaf with such ease and purpose that I looked a fool as I grabbed a handful of air.

The old man wore rags that covered his head and body. He began to turn around. As he did, his back slowly straightened until I faced a man who was a full three inches taller than I. He was not bent or gnarled or old. On the contrary, this man was close to my age and had shoulders as broad as a horse. His arms were defined and powerful. One could even see strength in his jaw as he removed the cloth that covered his head.

A man's eyes give away the story of his character, my father once told me. I forced myself to gaze into the eyes of the stranger. I felt as though he had already questioned my eyes for my character. His eyes burned like fire. They penetrated into the very depths of my soul. They were not eyes of hate or malice—far from it. I saw power yet meekness, forceful-ness yet gentleness, discipline yet compassion. I had never seen eyes like his!

He stretched forth his hand with the loaf of bread and offered it to me. I slowly took it from him.

"Tell me, Cedric," the stranger said in a rich voice, "what do you hope for?"

My mind was fuzzy. I heard the hungry cry of one of the children beside me. How selfish I felt. I was ready to rob an old man of his bread, and instead he gave me the very thing I'd hoped to take.

I knelt down to the child and gave her the loaf of bread. "I'm sorry I haven't more to give you," I told the child's mother.

I turned to the stranger once more. "I am a man of little hope, sir. The kingdom becomes more dreary every day. The people are starving, and the Noble Knights are the only ones who fare well. What is there to hope for? Were I foolish enough to hope, it would be that Arrethtrae was a kingdom free from hunger. A kingdom of truth, justice, and honor. A kingdom where men may serve the King as knights though only common blood flows through their veins, where each man's character, not his family name, determines his worth. No, hopes and dreams you will not find in my heart, for I am too acquainted with disappointment already. If you're looking for dreams, William here is the one to talk to."

"And what are your dreams, William?" the stranger asked as he turned toward him.

William seemed as taken aback by the stranger's gaze as I had been. "You are clothed as a peasant, though you hardly look the role. Tell me who you are, sir, and I shall tell you my dreams."

"I am a man from a distant land," the stranger said. "What are your dreams, William?"

William paused. "I dream of becoming a knight and serving my King as the Noble Knights do."

"And would you also pass out scraps of food to the poor as the Noble Knights do?"

"I *am* the poor, sir. I would never forget these people or their demise. I would defend my King and serve His people."

"Well spoken, gentlemen. Do not despair. The King knows the plight of His people in Arrethtrae. I bid you farewell, 'Cedric of Little Hope' and 'William of Dreams.'"

With that, the stranger turned and disappeared into the throng of people.

"Well, William," I said, "it looks as though you are not alone in your dreamworld."

"That man is more than a dreamer, and you know it. His peasant clothes don't fool me. There was something about that man!"

"Yes, yes, I'm sure he runs a dreamers guild you could join." I laughed and slapped William on the back.

There was *something about that man,* I thought.

CHAPTER TWO

THE UNLIKELY KNIGHT

 The days went by, and my mind kept returning to the encounter with the stranger from a distant land. *Who was he?*

"I hear the Noble Knights are training in the square this afternoon," William said as we lifted our day's catch onto the dock. "Let's go watch for a bit."

"It's all for show," I said. "We've seen them sword fight a hundred times."

"I know, but seeing how grandly they handle a sword gives me comfort when I think of the Dark Knight and his desire to conquer this kingdom someday."

"Yes, I suppose you're right," I said. "Let's finish up and make an early day of it."

On our way to the square, we detoured to Leinad's home to check on him.

"What do you think of Leinad?" I asked William as we neared the small cottage.

"I don't think I can answer that, Cedric. Calling him crazy doesn't fit, and yet his delusions of past adventures are absurd."

"I know what you mean," I said.

We knocked on Leinad's door. "Sir Leinad, may we enter?" I asked through the closed door.

There was no answer. I called to him again. Silence. I opened the door, hoping to find him asleep but dreading worse. He was not asleep nor was he anywhere in the home.

"Let's check down by the stream," I said with some urgency. "Maybe he fell while getting water."

Leinad was nowhere to be found. At the stream's edge, an ominous thought invaded my mind. I grabbed William's arm.

"The sword!" we said in unison and ran back to Leinad's home. We burst through the door and looked for the chest. It was in the corner and still closed, but I saw finger marks in the dust on its lid. I knelt down before the chest, hesitant, hoping not to find what I knew I would. The hinges creaked as I lifted the lid and gazed inside.

The cloth was open, and the sword was gone!

My heart sank, and William placed his hand on my shoulder. "I'm sorry, Cedric," he said. "There is a chance he is still alive."

I fought back tears and tried to convince myself that William was right. After all, there was no sign of a struggle, no body, and no blood.

"Maybe the sword was stolen while he was away," I said. "He could have gone into the city for provisions.

Although he is old, he is quite determined. Let's get to the city square and start looking there."

We entered the city, and I was anxious and disturbed. The mystery of Leinad's disappearance weighed heavily on my mind as we arrived at our destination. A large oak tree identified the center of the square. The people were already gathering to see the Noble Knights in action. Before long, thousands of people had assembled. The Noble Knights comprised one hundred of the strongest, bravest men in the kingdom. I had to admit that they looked to be an awesome force to reckon with. Their armor glistened and the horses stamped their pride at belonging to such a gallant force. The swords were a sight to behold. Each of these knights carried a sword that was the envy of all men. Their swords were the mark of their knighthood, a testament to their skill as swordsmen.

William and I searched the crowd and nearby shops in search of Leinad, but he was nowhere to be found. My hope faded, but I was determined to search the entire city if necessary.

The training of the Noble Knights began and I watched, but my mind found no rest from the mystery of Leinad's disappearance.

Each knight fought another to determine who was the better swordsman. Minutes into each duel, the better swordsman was obvious. The defeated knight would kneel in submission before his victor. Fifty were eliminated in the first round—then twenty-five. Swords screamed through the air and clashed with great force until one knight remained.

The Noble Knight Kifus always won. He was truly the best in the entire kingdom, and he proved it time after time. The people cheered as the Noble Knights encircled Kifus and knelt in honor.

"Thief!" yelled a man behind me, near a line of shops that bordered the square.

I turned and saw an enraged shop owner gripping the arm of a girl.

"Thief—she's stealing my bread!" he yelled again.

He grabbed her basket and opened it for all to see. A single loaf of bread was inside. She was guilty, and a hundred witnesses knew it.

The disturbance brought the attention of Kifus and the Noble Knights. They were clearly upset with the interruption of their ritual, but the shop owner dragged the girl into the opening. She tried to cover her face and resist, but it was pointless.

I had seen her on the streets before. She was a little younger than I, and she was pretty. Her auburn hair was mildly curly and hung below her shoulders. Though the faint, torn remnants of a dress revealed her extreme poverty, it was clear that she tried to keep herself as respectable looking as possible.

"Please...no!" She pleaded with the man as her slender form twisted in an attempt to escape the humiliation.

How could she have lowered herself to stealing, even in her poverty? I wondered.

Kifus and the other Noble Knights moved toward the man and his captive.

"What is going on here?" Kifus asked with authority.

Kifus and the Noble Knights were the executors of the law. They judged and sentenced all serious disputes and crimes.

"I caught this thief stealing bread from my shop! Here is the proof," he said as he held forth her basket.

"Is this true?" Kifus asked the young woman.

"Yes, my lord. But I only—"

"Maggie! Maggie!" A panicked woman burst through the crowd and ran to the girl. "Please, sir," the woman exclaimed. "Maggie is my oldest daughter, and she stole the bread only to feed her younger brothers and sisters. Please let her go, Lord Kifus!"

"The law is very clear," Kifus said. "Anyone caught stealing will lose their right hand! There are no exceptions...not even for your daughter."

"I have no way of providing for the children," the mother said, tears streaming down her face. "I have already lost one child to poor health and sickness. Maggie is a good girl. I will serve to repay this man. Please show mercy!"

Kifus looked at the woman and her daughter and then at the crowd.

"The law must be fulfilled. It is our Code that must be followed," he declared. "Stretch forth her arm on this tree stump!"

One knight peeled the girl from her mother's arms and brought her to the stump. Another knight restrained the mother as she clutched her bosom in anguish.

"No!" she screamed.

The knight held the girl while another wrapped a leather strap around her wrist and stretched her arm across the stump.

The crowd held its breath as the inescapable arm of the law readied to strike. Kifus drew back his sword and then started its powerful arc across the blue sky toward the delicate hand stretched out on the stump. Her fate seemed to be trapped in the steel jaws of the law.

A man to my right threw back a ragged cloak and I heard the *shing* of his sword as it left its scabbard. His motion was quick and smooth. The man drew forth a sword that had no equal, not even among the Noble Knights. Its beauty was unmatched and yet familiar. It gleamed so brightly in the sun that it was hard to look upon. Kifus's sword of judgment screamed through air and collided with this stranger's immovable sword of mercy—just above the maiden's wrist. The crowd exhaled in a unified gasp of astonishment.

Who dared to rescue this poor girl from the judgment of the Noble Knights? Who was this man who was either courageous or a fool? The moment seemed frozen in time. The stranger's magnificent sword, powered by mighty arms, held its position under the full strength of Kifus's cut.

The young lass opened her eyes and slowly turned her head to see the valiant face of her deliverer. Her countenance revealed shock, then gratitude, and finally fear, for the reprieve from judgment could only be temporary, and this brave soul would surely pay with his life.

"What is that fool doing?" William whispered in my ear.

No one had ever challenged the authority of any Noble Knight, let alone Kifus.

With his sword still in its protective position above the girl's wrist, the stranger slowly turned his head and locked eyes with Kifus. The rage in Kifus's eyes was evident to all.

"William," I whispered, "doesn't that peasant look familiar?"

"Yes, yes… It's the stranger we met on the street a few days ago! Why is he doing this?"

"I don't know, but look at that sword. It must be Leinad's!"

"Are you sure?"

I focused on the sword and tried to remember. It had been a long time since I'd laid eyes on Leinad's sword. If this man was a thief, he was a strange one. He was risking his life to save the life of a girl…and doing it with a stolen sword. I couldn't make sense of it.

"I can't be certain, but I think so," I whispered back. "In either case, I hope he's ready to die. It'll take more than a fancy sword to survive the wrath and skill of Kifus."

Kifus pulled back his sword and glared at the stranger, apparently stunned by the rebellious act of this peasant.

Kifus growled at the stranger, "That was a very stupid move, peasant! I don't know from whose castle you stole that sword, but I aim to run you through and return it to its rightful place among nobility. Prepare to die!"

The peasant raised his sword and took a swordsman's stance that caused even Kifus to hesitate. This man was no peasant. He emanated power!

Kifus charged. The stranger moved to the side with blinding speed, and his sword flashed like lightning to meet Kifus's charge. The impact nearly put Kifus on his face. He regained his balance and approached more cautiously now, and then he attacked again. The stranger met every blow and thrust with the perfection of a true master. He teased the Noble Knight Kifus as he maneuvered him at will.

We watched in amazement as the flashing swords clashed time after time.

Kifus must have thought he perceived an opening and lunged to finish the stranger, but the stranger parried and executed a bind on Kifus's sword with unmatched speed and power.

The fight was over. Kifus stood empty-handed, his sword beneath the foot of the stranger.

The crowd, along with the other knights, stood silent. I suspected that everyone had the same question on their minds as I had on mine: *Who was this man?*

The stranger had disgraced the entire force of the Noble Knights in front of all the people by defeating their best swordsman. I was still confused, but I knew that a man possessing such incredible skill and courage could hardly be a thief.

In a move of cowardice, two knights behind the stranger drew their swords.

"Behind you!" I shouted, but my warning was unnecessary. The stranger had already moved to meet their attack. No one standing in the square that afternoon would have believed that a single man could possess such craft as this swordsman were they not there to see it with their own eyes. Within minutes, one knight was without his sword, and the other was prone on the ground before the stranger, the tip of the magnificent sword at his throat.

"Release the girl," the stranger said.

The prone knight looked at Kifus and pleaded with his eyes.

Kifus nodded at the two knights who were restraining the young woman, and they released her. She was too stunned to move. I went to her and helped her gain her feet. She wiped away tears of deliverance as I guided her to her mother, who was still held in the grip of a Noble Knight. He finally released her, and Maggie collapsed into her mother's arms.

Kifus spoke. "You are not what you appear to be, sir. Tell us who you are and where you come from."

The stranger relaxed his sword. "I am the Son of the King of this kingdom, and I come from His palace in distant lands across the sea."

A low rumble flowed through the crowd. William came and stood by me.

"Could this be true, William?" I said. "Do you think He really is the King's Son?"

"I don't know," William said. "I want to believe it. Like I told you, there is definitely something about that man!"

"If You are the King's Son, give us a sign," Kifus called out. "Show us Your royal ring and robe. Where are Your servants, Your coaches, and the treasures worthy of a prince?"

"I can give no sign, save My skill as a swordsman and My duty to My Father," the stranger said.

"Nobility is more than wielding a sword, stranger. It is in the blood. This we know by the Code our King gave us," Kifus said. "We live by the Code!"

"You speak of the Code, yet you do not live by the Code

nor teach the people so that they may live by the Code. You dishonor the King by your actions. The Code of the King is not born in your blood but grown in your hearts. You feed the people morsels of food and keep them in subjection to your whims for the sake of power and control. That is not nobility—it is treachery!"

Never before had anyone dared speak such truth out loud. All that He said made perfect sense. The people were clearly moved as He spoke, and the Noble Knights appeared to grow more furious with every word.

"While you serve yourselves, the Dark Knight prepares this very day for battle against our kingdom," the stranger continued. He turned toward the crowd. "People of Arrethtrae, My Father has not forgotten you. I come to raise up an army of truth, justice, and honor. An army willing to fight and die for the good of the kingdom. An army willing to serve the people. An army that must someday fight the Dark Knight and his Shadow Warriors. I come in the name of the King! I come to serve Him and you. Follow Me and learn the true ways of the Code."

"You are a traitor to the King!" Kifus shouted. "I will not allow You to destroy His kingdom or His Code!"

The King's Son turned toward Kifus. He raised His magnificent sword at him and the Noble Knights. "*You* have defiled the Code and are not worthy to be called the King's Noble Knights. Be sure of this, I will accomplish My Father's will!"

His voice was overpowering. Kifus seemed to shrink from the rebuke.

The King's Son spoke to the people. "I have chosen men

among you worthy to serve the King. I do not offer a life of ease and comfort, but of sweat and blood. It will not be easy, but it will be noble!"

He moved toward the crowd and closer to us. Soon He was standing before William and me. I looked once more into those penetrating eyes. Was this really happening, or was I in some strange dream? Could this really be the King's Son? I knew in my heart that what He said was true; I saw it in His eyes. This was a man who would not lie. My gaze left His eyes and came to rest on the magnificent sword. It fit His hand as though it were part of Him. He followed my eyes.

"Cedric," I heard him say, "Leinad has done well in keeping My sword for this appointed day. Do not worry. Your friend is safe."

I believed Him and found relief in His words. But why He would entrust such a treasure as this sword to a crazy old man was still a mystery. The golden handle was inlaid with precious stones. Its double-edged blade shined like polished silver and was as sharp as a razor's edge. What a splendid sword it was.

I looked into His face again as He continued to speak. "Will you discover hope and follow Me to become a Knight of the Prince, Cedric?"

Me? Surely He was mistaken. "My Lord," I said, "I am but a poor peasant. I am not worthy. Surely You look for someone better than I?"

"No, Cedric, I have chosen you. I do not care about what you were or what you are, but about what you can become."

In my heart I knew I must answer one question: *Do I really believe this man is the Son of the King?* In an instant I knew the answer, and there was but one thing for me to do.

I knelt before the Prince. "I will follow You, my Lord."

"And you, William. Will you follow Me and discover your dreams?" He asked my friend.

"My life is Yours, my Prince," William said as he knelt beside me.

"Rise up, My friends, and come with Me." His firm hand was upon our shoulders.

We rose and followed Him through the crowd. The Prince stopped before certain men and bid them to follow Him. Most joined us, but some did not. The men He chose were anything but warriors. But who was I to talk? I knew nothing of the skill of sword fighting or knighthood. I had held a sword only once in my life, and it was the very sword that the Prince now carried. Leinad had let me hold it once when I was boy. His tale of the Sword of the King had captivated me, and holding it had made the story seem real. I believed him then, but had lost that childhood faith in my mature years. Now it all seemed to be happening just as Leinad had said. Maybe he wasn't as crazy as I had thought.

As we emerged from the crowd, twenty-five men, scruffy men, followed the Prince. The Noble Knights roared in laughter.

"So this is Your grand army to defeat the Dark Knight, aye, stranger?" Kifus sneered. "I'm sure Your King would be proud of such an awesome selection of knights to defend His kingdom."

The Prince showed no embarrassment at us as one might expect, but instead turned toward the knights one last time and spoke with authority. "On the appointed day, you will be judged for your treason, and I shall be that judge. My Father has given Me all authority over this kingdom. Be warned!"

That was the beginning of my life as an unlikely knight. It was a day that changed my life forever.

CHAPTER THREE

A DEADLY PLOT

Life was hard. Life was good. Most folks think this a contradiction, but I have learned that the hardest, most difficult times of my life caused the most growth in my character. At the very least, those hard times prepared me for a better future.

The Prince…

Were the Noble Knights to spend one honest day with Him, they would have realized how truly noble He is and that He is indeed the King's Son. He is better with the sword than any man, past or present, who has laid his hand upon a hilt. And yet He is not arrogant. His authority as a military commander is unquestioned, and yet He is not harsh. He does not hesitate to destroy evil at its root, and yet He is more compassionate than any man I've seen. He is the King's Son, and yet I have seen Him carry a poor old woman to her home when she was too weak to walk by herself. This is what the Noble Knights hate most about

Him—He is kind. He is the epitome of what they are not.

We learned the art of the sword from the Master Himself, a little each day. He was patient. We studied and worked and sweat. We all wanted to become like the Prince. There is a quality about Him that draws the good in heart. As we became more proficient, the Prince recruited more men to His army. They too were inept swordsmen at first, but the Master made warriors of them all. We were the Knights of the Prince.

The Noble Knights must have realized that this stranger was not going away. I was told that when they saw His influence over the people, their ridicule became concern. Soon their concern became a plot.

"William, how was your training today?" I asked as we walked up the narrow streets of Chessington toward the bread stand.

"Well, I've been working on some techniques the Prince showed me, but no matter how many times I practice, my skills pale in comparison to His."

"I understand. My best work seems a weak imitation of the Prince's."

We now wore the emblem of the Prince on our tunics. The swords and scabbards He gave us also bore His mark. We turned the corner and walked up a dimly lit street. The clink of our swords kept rhythm with our walk.

"Good sirs!" came a whisper from the dark.

Dark shadows usually hide dark deeds. We instinctively reached for our swords.

"Who goes there?" I said.

"I am but a servant boy. Please do not harm me," the small voice replied.

We could not see the boy, but fear was clearly in his voice.

"What do you want, lad?" William said.

"I serve in Lord Kifus's house, but I have seen how your leader cares for the people. I come to warn your leader. I overheard some of the knights talking of a plot to kill Him. Please warn Him. I must go."

We strained to see but only heard the quickened pace of bare feet on cobblestone diminishing to our left side.

"Do you think there is any merit to this warning?" William said. "Are the Noble Knights really that worried about the Prince that they would plot to kill Him?"

"That boy was scared. I believe the threat to be real, but plot or no plot, we must tell the Prince immediately."

We found the Prince resting beneath a sprawling tree on a knoll east of the city. This was a place of solitude He'd come to love.

"Good Prince!" I exclaimed. "I am sorry to disturb You, but we have news You must hear at once."

"Yes, Cedric," the Prince said. "Please tell Me your urgent news."

I caught my breath from the climb up the hill. "A young servant boy who serves in Kifus's house overheard talk of a plot to kill You! We were not able to validate the source but thought it wise to at least warn You."

The Prince did not seem uninterested, but He was not alarmed by our message.

"Do not worry, My friends. I am not through preparing you or My army. The King's work must be completed. I will not allow Kifus or any of the Noble Knights to interfere."

"But my Lord," William said, "shouldn't we prepare somehow in the event that there is truth in this warning?"

"Cedric. William. There is coming a day when I must return to My Father's distant kingdom."

"My Lord, may we come with You to serve You there?" I asked.

"No, Cedric. You and the Knights of the Prince must continue what I have started here. Upon you I place My trust. There is one coming who is far more destructive than Kifus or his knights. Leinad warned the people, but their apathy has left them weak."

William and I locked eyes in astonishment. *Leinad?* I thought. *My crazy old companion wasn't really crazy? That means that all of those bizarre stories were—*

"Yes, Leinad was highly favored by the King," the Prince said in response to our obvious amazement. "He was a mighty and faithful knight, but the kingdom slowly began to ignore him and My Father's warning until Leinad was all but forgotten. Now the Dark Knight is strong and anxious to conquer Arrethtrae. The kingdom is in peril. That is why you must continue to recruit and train men to fight the Dark Knight. He is evil and powerful. When you have established our army of truth, justice, and honor, the Dark Knight will come to destroy you."

He paused for us to digest what He'd just said. It was hard to hear this plan. What strategy was this? Why would He leave us when we needed Him most?

"But do not fear," the Prince continued. "I will come back for you and bring you into My Father's kingdom to complete your training. Then we will return to Arrethtrae to utterly destroy the Dark Knight and his Shadow Warriors once and for all. I will lead you to certain victory! I will be King here, and you will help Me rule."

He seemed so sure of Himself and of the future. It was clear He knew His enemies well, but I had yet to see even the best-laid plan executed without a few major flaws. Yet there was something about this man.

"You must remain true to the Code. It will carry and preserve you when you think you cannot go on. Do not just memorize the Code…*live* the Code. Will you trust Me, gentlemen?"

I glanced toward William. His face was solemn, but his eyes were set on the Prince. We had seen the strength of the Prince when all odds were against Him. Why should we doubt Him now?

"We trust You though it cost our very lives, my Lord," William said.

We knelt before the Prince to confirm our vow.

"Rise and eat with Me, good knights," the prince said, and He offered bread and fruit.

While we ate, the Prince spoke. "Listen closely. Besides the Knights of the Prince, I have established a secret force in the land composed of true and valiant knights from My Father's distant kingdom. These men are skilled in the art of the sword and in the art of stealth and disguise. My Silent Warriors will help you in your most desperate times when I am not with you. When you call, 'The King reigns—and His Son,' should any be near, they will come to your aid."

"Are there many of the Silent Warriors in the kingdom, my Prince?" I asked.

"More than your eyes will see, Cedric. They are mighty men. I once led them in battle against the Dark Knight and his Shadow Warriors many years ago in My Father's kingdom. The battle was fierce. We defeated them but did not conquer. The Dark Knight and most of his Shadow Warriors escaped. That is why they are preparing to attack this kingdom. They want *revenge!*"

CHAPTER FOUR

A DESPERATE FIGHT

 Our training continued each day. Once we mastered a particular technique, the Prince would challenge us with a new, more difficult one.

On that day I was in just such a training session with a fellow knight and parried his oncoming thrust to the left. "Rob, your skill with the sword is impressive. You've improved dramatically since we last fenced."

Rob caught my vertical cut and countered with a quick side slice. "Aye, and yours as well, Cedric. Remember though, it was only the third day of training when we first took up our clumsy swords and flung them at each other."

Rob had also been one of the first men chosen by the Prince on that spectacular day in the square seven months ago. Rob was offensive to me at first. He was rude and brash, but I quickly saw a genuinely kind heart within him. The more I got to know him, the more I liked him. His curly red hair and fair complexion seemed always accompanied by a boyish grin.

"Yes, I remember well. The Prince is more than a teacher, for it took a miracle to make swordsmen out of us," I said as I caught his slice and countered with my own.

"He is indeed a miracle worker, in more ways than one," Rob said.

"What do you mean?"

Rob parried my thrust this time, and the flats of our swords met midway.

"Well, haven't you seen the joy on the faces of the people?" Rob said. "He has promised to heal this country and restore the people's dignity, and they believe Him! I know this much—if any man alive can do it, He'll be the one."

We finished the session, and our swords found rest in our scabbards.

"I believe you're right, Rob," I said. "The Prince seems to have all the ingredients to make just such a thing happen."

THAT EVENING, WILLIAM AND I passed by a small shop on our way home. We heard a ruckus from within and decided to investigate. As we opened the door, a part of me wished we had chosen to walk on and ignore this place.

Two other occupants were inside the room. One, who I presumed to be the owner of the shop, was white and pale. I do not know if the lack of blood to his face was the result of fear or because of the large hand that nearly encircled his neck. The other occupant owned the threatening hand, and a large hulking body to go with it. His back was to us, but it was enough to know he commanded enormous strength. He heard us enter and turned his head.

"If you want to live, leave this place!" His voice was deep and gruff, the mere sound of it as threatening as his form.

It was then that I noticed that the shop owner's feet were not touching the ground. Pain joined with the fear I first saw on his face.

"Release this man or face our swords," I said as boldly as my own fear allowed.

I saw the grip on the shop owner tighten slightly before the beast of a man threw him into a corner as though he were a rag doll.

"Don't move!" the man said to the shop owner.

He slowly turned to face us, revealing all of his horrific grandeur. He stood nearly seven feet tall. His stringy hair hung to his shoulders, partly hiding a deep scar that swept from his left cheekbone down to his chin. His eyes were dark and filled with poisonous hate. His neck joined his shoulders and chest in a mass of muscle. His arms were as thick as a young cedar tree. The hand that had encircled a neck just seconds ago now held a gleaming sword.

But even this did not chill me as much as what I saw next. His tunic bore the mark of the Dark Knight…he was a Shadow Warrior!

So this is a glimpse of the evil force spoken of by the Prince. I prayed it would not be my last glimpse of life itself.

His voice was thick with indignation. "You will regret that you chose to interfere. Now you die!"

He attacked us so violently and forcefully that I feared

he would spill our blood with hardly a fight. His blows were incredibly powerful. We retreated slightly to regain ourselves and spread apart to divert his attack. William caught a slice across his arm that bled but was not deep. I pressed an attack to bring the brute off William.

How could we escape with our lives let alone bring justice to this criminal?

William brought some hope to our cause as I saw him advance with a combination the Prince had taught us. In the throes of the Shadow Warrior's fierce attack, I was so preoccupied with defending myself that I had neglected to rely on the training the Prince had so diligently given us for just such an encounter.

We tightened our positions and ever so slowly began a methodical advance that soon had the Shadow Warrior on the defensive. His eyes spewed hate, but I saw surprise momentarily cross his face. He renewed his fighting and we gave, but only temporarily. Advance—retreat. Advance—retreat. Were it not for two of us versus one of him, the fight would have ended abruptly. Instead, it wore on.

The shop owner was still a puddle in the corner. I did not know if he was dead or if he feared that the Shadow Warrior was toying with us and thus dared not move.

For all we were worth, William and I could not bring this brute down. We were tiring, but the Shadow Warrior's energy seemed inexhaustible. I knew we were slipping. I'm sure the Shadow Warrior knew it too.

"You fight like my enemy of old," he growled at us. "Tell me who your trainer is before I end your miserable lives."

A floorboard creaked at the entrance of the shop, and my heart sank. Had another Shadow Warrior entered from behind? Was this to be our end?

"I am!" came the familiar voice of the Prince in response to the Shadow Warrior's question.

At last, I thought. *With three of us, we will have a chance of defeating the massive warrior.* What a foolish thought it was.

For the first time, I saw fear on the face of the Shadow Warrior. Not just a glimmer of fear, but fear that comes from deep within and stays. His fight immediately left him. The once flashing, powerful sword now hung limply in his hands.

"I know who You are, Son of the King," the Shadow Warrior said with a quaver in his voice.

William and I slowly backed off in amazement. This Shadow Warrior could defeat any one of the Noble Knights within seconds, including Kifus, yet the mere sight of the Prince turned him into a cowering fool. At that moment I began to realize how truly awesome the Son of the King was.

The Prince placed His hand on His majestic sword. The Shadow Warrior withdrew two steps, his sword still lowered.

"Let me live," came a weak, gruff plea.

"Lay down your sword and go!" the Prince said.

The Shadow Warrior did not hesitate. He dropped his sword and moved quickly toward the door. His eyes never left the Prince until he was safely in the street. He turned and ran into the darkness.

The shop owner threw himself at the feet of the Prince. "Thank You, my Lord. You have saved my life this night!"

"What is your name?" the Prince asked.

"My name is Barrett, my Lord."

"Rise up, Barrett." The Prince lifted Barrett by his arm. "Tell Me, how did you fall victim to the likes of this gruesome man?"

Only now was the color coming back to Barrett's face. He started to talk but coughed and choked on his words. I offered him water as he tried to regain some composure.

Barrett was slightly shorter than I with an average build. His coffee-colored hair had receded to the top of his head, and his face was clean shaven. His eyes darted nervously left and right. I wondered if this was a lifelong mannerism or a consequence of his recent near-death experience. Barrett was ready to try once again.

"A few months ago, this same man entered my shop and offered to buy my geese and fish at a price higher than I could get from anyone in the city. His only demand was that I tell no one about him or our exchange. He seemed fair enough, so I took his offer. A few days later, he returned with nearly the same offer, so I agreed. This continued for some time, but each time his price got lower and his demeanor became more fierce. Before long, he demanded the food at a fraction of the market price and threatened me and my family if I didn't agree."

Barrett paused and took another sip of water. He took a deep breath and continued.

"Eventually, I was giving him the food, and he was also demanding money. I told the Noble Knights, but they seemed too afraid to even confront him. I do believe he would have killed me tonight had these gentlemen not intervened. Thank you for your bravery, kind sirs. Please take this money in payment for your services."

The shop owner offered a bag that jingled with the sound of coins—coins the Shadow Warrior had apparently hoped to steal.

"We accept your thanks but not your payment, Barrett," I said. "We cannot receive money for doing what is honorable and just."

Barrett turned toward the Prince, and fear surfaced once again on his face. "My Lord, how can I be sure this brute will not return?"

"If he returns, Barrett, you can be sure he will not return alone. He will bring other warriors more fierce and wretched than himself with him," the Prince said.

Barrett looked desperate.

"There is only one way you can protect yourself and your family. Follow Me, and I will train you, equip you, and protect you."

"I will follow You this very night, my Lord," said Barrett with renewed hope in his eyes that only moments ago were full of fear and desperation.

It was clear that I still had much to learn from the Prince!

CHAPTER FIVE

MASTER OF THE SWORD

 We were not experts with the sword by any stretch of the imagination. However, the Prince felt we had learned enough of the sword to add armor to our training. On one particularly warm afternoon, He chose to teach a few of us how to use the shield.

"It is your shield that will protect you when your enemies fire their flaming arrows at you," the Prince said. "It will stop the deadly blows of their axes and swords. I gave each of you a shield. Take good care of it, for the enemy may strike when you least expect it."

Two hours passed. At first, the shield seemed awkward and clumsy in my hand. But soon, it was natural to hold and use. I enjoyed the feeling of security it provided.

I was so engrossed with my training that I did not even see them coming. Three of the Noble Knights descended from a hill toward the south of us. Their swords were drawn, and they attacked quickly. Although I was surprised, the Prince was not. He was always ready. He had already positioned Himself for the onslaught with His shining sword in hand.

These Noble Knights were three of the best. I recognized them from the training they conducted frequently in the square. My initial reaction was to flee. There were four trainees, and we were no match for the Noble Knights. Not yet anyway. Despite my instinct to run, I raised my sword for the fight, as did my companions.

"Stand down, gentlemen," the Prince said. "This is my fight."

It was clear He was right, for the Noble Knights focused exclusively on Him. We did not seem to pose a threat to them at all. We watched, but did not sheathe our swords. We had pledged our lives to the King's Son, and this could be the day to make good our vows.

"Cedric, your sword," the Prince called.

I tossed my sword fifteen feet to the Prince. As my sword was midflight, the Prince turned to His right to engage the first approaching knight. A split second later, the Prince snatched the flying sword blindly with his left hand and brought it to bear on the second knight. His timing and reaction were perfect.

The knights fought with cautious tenacity, for the Prince's skill as a swordsman was legendary. They tried to encircle Him, but the Prince moved quickly toward a hill that rose up out of the flat ground we were training on. The rise was steep enough that a man could not easily climb it or fight from its slope. With the steep terrain at His back, the Prince forced the Noble Knights to engage Him head-on.

The swords flashed through the air with deadly cuts. I studied the face of the Master as He fought, but I found no panic or fear at all. His jaw was set, and His eyes were focused, as though they were weapons themselves.

"You have committed crimes of treason against the King," one of the knights said. "We are here to end Your traitorous deeds!"

"If you truly knew the King, you would also know Me and why I am here," the Prince said. "You have become ignorant and foolish in your ways. I am here to reestablish My Father's kingdom of honor, truth, and justice…to restore the true meaning of the Code in Arrethtrae."

The three knights formed a semicircle around the Prince. His predicament seemed hopeless, but I knew not to underestimate His skill. He had surprised me many times before. He parried with His left sword and attacked with His right.

I thought that surely with His concentration split on three Noble Knights, He would make a mistake and it would soon be over. But the knights found no flaw. To this day I have never seen a sword fly so swiftly. He met each thrust with absolute precision. The harder the Noble Knights tried, the quicker His sword flew to meet each stroke.

The knight to the Prince's right made the first mistake. I suppose he thought he saw an opening and thrust forth with all his might, fully expecting to feel his sword meet flesh and bone. The Prince finished glancing a vertical cut from the center knight and met the knight's thrust from the front, causing the sword to pass behind His back. The knight was now overextended and slightly off balance. The Prince struck a blow to his head with the gold handle of His sword, which knocked him to the ground unconscious.

The two remaining knights pressed harder, appearing eager to finish the fight. One knight sent a high vertical cut toward the Prince at the same time his partner launched a knee level slice. The Prince pulled His left sword off the knight delivering the slice to the knee and met the vertical cut from the front in the crux of a cross formed by His two swords as He jumped to escape the knee cut. The low sword passed beneath Him, and the Prince planted a forceful heel into the chest of the knight on His left. The knight stumbled back and fell.

The Prince landed and turned on the remaining knight with both swords. Stark fear clouded the Noble Knight's face. He put forth his sword to defend himself from the impact of two swords, each one commanded by arms more powerful and skilled than his own. In one powerful blow, the Prince crosscut both swords with such force that they sheared the knight's sword in two!

The Noble Knight stood dumbfounded and afraid. The knight that had fallen was now on his feet and slowly moving toward the Prince and the sword-less knight. The Prince placed a sword at the neck of the knight he'd just beaten and moved him toward the approaching knight with the edge of His blade.

"Drop your sword," the Prince said.

I knew these knights were not used to being humbled, but better judgment prevented the knight from meeting a senseless death. He dropped his sword.

"Take your unconscious friend and leave," the Prince said. "And tell Kifus that he must do his own dirty work in the future."

As they turned to pick up the other knight, one of the knights turned back toward the Prince. "Are you truly the King's Son?" he asked.

The Prince studied his face and said, "What does your heart tell you?"

The Noble Knight was silent. Then they all turned and left.

CHAPTER SIX

THE TEAR

 William, Rob, and I walked with the Prince through the streets of the poorest quarter of Chessington one morning before our training began. The crisp air and fresh sunrise were overshadowed by the absence of joy. The sounds of playful, giggling children had been replaced by moans of hunger as they rummaged for a scrap of food. The early morning song of motherhood had been exchanged for the wail of a suckling babe with no milk to drink. The poverty of Chessington had grown to encompass thousands of its citizens, and the Noble Knights did not seem to notice or care.

I longed to leave these wretched streets, for I could not bear the pain. But the Master lingered in solemn silence.

"My Lord," I said softly, "shouldn't we be on our way to begin our training?" I'd hoped to move on to the country, away from such despair.

As the Prince turned toward me, I saw deep sadness in

His face. A tear fell from His cheek and was swallowed by the dust at our feet.

"Your training is here today, Cedric," the Prince said. "Bring the rest of My knights here as quickly as you can."

"Yes, my Prince," I said.

We left at once and found the rest of our brothers at the training site.

When we returned, I was once again astonished by what I saw. The Prince was sitting on a stump with children all around Him listening to a story He was telling. Two were sitting on His lap. Children! Children covered in dirt and filth. Why would the mightiest warrior in the kingdom waste time with children? It seemed like such a contradiction. Power, might, strength, and wisdom matched equally with kindness, compassion, and gentleness, all in one man—the King's Son.

He finished the story before addressing us. "Gentlemen, you will feed these people."

We looked at each other rather stupidly, and I was trying to decide if I'd heard right.

"How many people, my Lord?" Rob asked.

"All of them."

Although I had seen many amazing things done by the Prince, I don't believe I was alone in thinking that He had crossed the line of rationality. There were thousands of poor people, maybe more. How could we possibly provide for such a mass of hunger?

"My Lord," William said, "I told You I will never forget the poor, and I won't. We will gladly feed them if there is some way, but You are asking the impossible."

"Today, William, you will begin to fulfill your duty in remembering the poor. You all will, for this is the meaning of the Code. Go to the docks. There you will find ships full of provisions sent from My Father at My request. Organize yourselves in teams of two, and deliver these provisions to each home. Do not miss a single household."

It was just as the Prince said. All the knights worked day and night until every home had food. It was glorious work. None of the knights complained at the labor but instead stepped with light feet as each delivery was made.

The people wept with gratefulness. We wept with joy. Children jumped with glee at such a grand gift.

Here was Compassion that acted. I had never seen its equal.

CHAPTER SEVEN

NO ESCAPE

We had learned much. In nine short months, the Prince had raised us from the depths of poverty-torn peasants to the heights of knighthood. The Prince spent as much time teaching us how to honor the Code and the King as He did on how to handle our swords.

As we learned more from Him, we learned more about Him. There was something divine in His nature. I feared Him for His power. I revered Him for His skill. I followed Him for His wisdom. But I served Him for His goodness.

How was it possible that one man could touch another man's life and change it so drastically? I was no longer Cedric the peasant. I was Cedric, Knight of the Prince. This honor did not come because I was able to make a knight of myself, but because the Prince chose to make a knight of me.

Why me? The question would not leave my mind.

The sun scorched the countryside, but we pressed on with our training. We broke midafternoon to quench our thirst and eat bread. Beneath the shade of a small grove of trees, the Prince spoke.

"Gentlemen, I am pleased with your training. You are all capable warriors now. You must fully understand the meaning of the Code and bury it in your hearts. To live by the Code is to love and serve the King, and to love and serve each other. Without the Code, your newfound skills with the sword are meaningless and will eventually destroy you. Remember what I have taught you. You must recruit and teach others. My words will guide you in the future."

Sadness fell upon me as I listened to His words. Why did they sink my heart so? Surely this was not the end.

"My time with you is over." The Prince spoke the words I had been dreading, though He had warned us of this day.

Shock and fear swept over me, and whispers and murmurs rose in volume around me.

"What do You mean, my Prince?" a fellow knight asked.

"Your training is complete. I have received word from My Father and must return to His kingdom. One day, I will send for all of you, and you will come and feast with Me in His kingdom. But for now your work is here."

"My Lord, we have so much more to learn from You," another knight said. "We cannot possibly be prepared to take on the Dark Knight and his—"

A thunderous noise came from the north and grew louder with each passing moment. No, it was from the west. No, it surrounded us from all sides. The sound of the pounding of horses' hooves engulfed us. We drew swords and looked for a place of retreat but found none. Fear came as quickly as the horses.

One hundred Noble Knights with their mounts soon encircled our position. The countenance of Kifus made clear that his intention was war. We were outnumbered nearly four to one, and they were mounted.

Today we die, I thought.

"Be still!" came the confident voice of the Prince.

"Today your lies and blasphemies end," Kifus said. "Your death and the deaths of your petty servants will restore order to this kingdom once and for all!"

"Remember, My knights," the Prince said to us, "your fight is with the Dark Knight and his Shadow Warriors. This is not your time."

The Prince walked toward Kifus without His sword drawn. If this battle were to happen, I knew we would all die. Our fight would be noble but futile. Only the Prince had the power and skill to defeat these vicious opponents. At least He would survive. I knew this to be true.

Midway in the gulf between Kifus and our men, the Prince stopped and spoke. "Kifus, your grievance is with Me, not My men. Spare the needless spilling of blood and let My men leave peacefully. I will come to you unarmed as your captive."

The Prince had the power to live, yet He offered His life for us? Why didn't He heed our warning? How could a man this wise allow such a thing to happen?

I did not know what to feel. Gratitude, anger, humiliation, and fear meshed together, leaving only a feeling of impending defeat.

Kifus sat smugly on his horse and seemed to enjoy the moment of power and control. He'd won. Revenge for his humiliation at the sword of this impostor obviously tasted sweet, though I knew deep down he was relieved that he did not have to face the Prince's sword again.

"So let it be," Kifus said. "Make way!"

Behind us, the circle of Noble Knights broke open to allow us passage. No one moved. How could we abandon the Master we had come to love, trust, and serve?

"Gentlemen, you must leave," the Prince said. "Remember the Code. Live the Code. Continue the Code, or all that I have done is for naught. Leave in peace."

One by one, the Knights of the Prince turned and walked through the circle of certain death. My own cowardice caused me to turn and leave. Once beyond the break, we ran like frightened, homeless children.

I was ashamed!

From the crest of a hill, I peered and saw a dreadful scene unfold. The deadly circle of Noble Knights hesitated in their advance as the Prince drew His sword. He looked down at its beauty and then to the hills.

Kifus reached for his sword, but it was not needed. The Prince drew back and threw the magnificent sword into the sky. It slowly rotated end over end, and the sun occasionally gleamed off its steel as it arched high above the Noble Knights and beyond the clearing. It disappeared far into the thick trees and brush of the forested hills.

He had chosen a silent surrender. The Noble Knights collapsed on him. The powerful hands of the Prince were empty.

CHAPTER EIGHT

A TIME
TO WEEP

 I tried to awaken from this bad dream, but morning did not come. Our small group of would-be knights had scattered. We feared for our lives now. Once they had eliminated the Prince, nothing could stop the Noble Knights from hunting us down and executing us for treason. Our strength and confidence abandoned us when we abandoned the Prince.

I was back in my peasant rags, attempting to hide. Now I was poor, hungry, and hunted. Worst of all, I was alone. It was a loneliness that surely would last forever.

I sat beneath the shade of an awning just off the street where I had first met "the stranger." So much had transpired since then. Two men were talking as they passed by.

"The hangin' is this afternoon," I heard an old man say to another.

"I knew that stranger was an impostor all along," the

second man said. "Kifus should've strung 'im up a long time ago."

"Maybe, but I didn't see you complainin' when He was handin' food to ya!"

"Hey, anytime there's a free lunch to be had, I ain't gonna complain. But it don't mean I believed what He said." He spit to emphasize his disgust.

"Still, I don't see how such a man…"

The words drifted into the distance along with my thoughts.

I began questioning my own belief in the Prince. If He truly was the King's Son, why would His life stop at the end of a rope tied by the very men sworn to serve the King? Nothing made sense anymore. My mind ran through thick fog searching for clarity, but found none. I wanted the earth to open up and swallow all evidence of Cedric the peasant.

THE SQUARE WAS PACKED with people. Near the center was the large oak tree. I forced my eyes to search, and I found it—from one of the large limbs hung a rope. I found a corner between two buildings and faded into the shadows, as did my heart.

Kifus led his death procession of Noble Knights around the perimeter of the square, displaying the Prince as though He were some prize catch of the day. His hands were bound, and His head was bruised and bleeding, as was His back. My soul was tormented to see Him this way.

Some people were laughing and jeering; some were crying.

Why? Why is this happening? I could not bear it any longer and hid my face in the brick and mortar of the wall. I stole a last glance and caught the eyes of the Prince looking my way as the procession passed.

Even now, on the verge of His death, His eyes held no fear. What I saw was tender compassion. The true power and strength of this man was in His great ability to love in spite of all tragedy. Now I fully understood the Code. The Prince lived the Code. The Prince *was* the Code.

My doubts were gone, but my despair was not. I felt so helpless. He had saved my life once. Now He was dying for me, and there was nothing I could do but watch.

Kifus led the Prince to the oak tree, placed Him on a horse, and slipped the rope about His neck.

Where was the army of the King to save His Son from death? Didn't He care? Did He even know the peril His Son was in? Where were the Silent Warriors?

Kifus spoke loudly for all to hear. "People of Arrethtrae, this man is guilty of treason against the King and against you. He has lied to you and misled you. He brings chaos to the kingdom. Today, justice is served!"

Kifus slapped the horse, and the Prince hanged. No army, no help, only silence—a silence that gripped the people as we watched our hope of a better kingdom die with this man.

I turned and ran to the hills. The trees and sky were blurred by my tears. I ran until I felt that my lungs would burst. At last I collapsed beneath a sprawling tree. The tall grass swallowed me, and I wept bitterly.

It truly was over.

CHAPTER NINE

A NEW BEGINNING

 The sun was nearing the horizon before I found enough energy to move. My tears were gone and so was my hope. I raised myself to my knees and wiped away the trails of dirt on my face. *What now?* I wondered.

My head hurt and my soul was empty.

Still on my knees, I looked over the grass and brush and realized that my blind run had brought me to familiar country. Our training area was nearby. I moved to stand up, but my eyes caught a glimpse of the unbelievable. Just an arm's length away was the Prince's sword, its blade embedded in the soft soil.

I stood and pulled the sword from the ground and held it before me in open palms. The memories of the Prince came back to me like a flood.

"Why did You have to die?" I asked out loud, certain that I would never find an answer.

🔱 🔱 🔱

"Cedric, what are we going to do?" William tried to break into my muddled thoughts as I stared at nothing.

Most of the Knights of the Prince had been scattered, but we had managed to meet with a dozen fellow knights in secret. Barrett's shop had a back room with no windows. We locked the doors and spoke in hushed tones.

"Yes, Cedric, what happens now?" Rob asked. "Do we try to get to another city or flee the kingdom altogether?"

"No," I finally said. "First we must honor the memory of the Prince and give Him a proper burial."

"What!" Rob said. "Are you mad, Cedric? The Noble Knights have purposely left His body hanging from that tree as a message to all the people. If we try to take Him down, we'll be found out and killed immediately!"

"Not if we go now, Rob," I said. "It's the middle of the night, and we can be quick about it. They have posted only two guards. Some of us can set up a diversion while the others cut down the body. This is something we must do. They have disgraced the Prince and the King!"

A long moment of silence was my only answer. I moved toward the door hoping that at least a few men would follow. Some did.

William, Rob, Barrett, and I stealthily moved from street to street, making our way toward the square. The others stayed behind.

"How are we going to do this with only four of us?" William whispered as we crossed our last street before reaching the square.

"I'm not sure," I whispered back. "Let's take a look at the square from behind that brick wall by those trees. We'll form a plan from there."

We moved carefully to the low brick wall. Our backs were completely covered by the thick trees on one side, and the brick wall protected the other. From this vantage point, we could easily see the entire square, including the large oak tree in the center, thanks to the light of a half-moon.

Something was wrong.

My eyes were fully adjusted to the dim light, but I could not see the body of the Prince. I forced my eyes to decipher what must be an illusion caused by shadows. As I focused more carefully, I could see the rope, but His body was gone.

"What did they do with His body?" I asked the other three.

"I don't know," Barrett said. "But look on the ground beneath the tree. The guards are either asleep or knocked out cold."

"I don't like this, Cedric," Rob said. "Let's get out of here before we're found out and hanged ourselves."

© Marcella Johnson

At that moment, we froze and my heart nearly stopped beating. Just a few feet away, on the other side of the brick wall, stood a large man. In our earnest desire to see what had happened at the oak tree, this fellow must have quietly made his way to our cover and was now upon us.

"Why do you look for the Prince here?" the man said in a thick accent I'd never heard before.

"We came to bury the body," I said. "Can you tell us where they've taken the body, sir? Where is the Prince?"

The large fellow gave a slight chuckle. "Do not worry. The Prince will find you!"

With the speed of a cat, he jumped the brick wall and disappeared into the shadows of some trees. I thought I heard a scrape of steel on brick as he crossed the wall. He was gone as quickly as he appeared.

"What is that supposed to mean?" William asked.

"I don't know," I said. "But I agree with Rob. It's time to leave this place. Let's get back to Barrett's shop."

"What do you mean someone's taken the body?" asked Jonathan, one of the other knights in Barrett's back room. "Surely it must have been the Noble Knights. No one is foolish enough to try such a risky task—present company excluded, of course."

"Look, if it was the Noble Knights, then why were two guards sleeping beneath an empty oak tree in the middle of the square?" Rob asked. "The guards must have been over-taken and knocked out. Then someone took the body. I don't know why, but maybe it was the large fellow who nearly scared us out of our wits."

"What large fellow?" a fellow knight asked.

"Just as we were getting ready to leave, a large—"

I stopped midsentence. Footsteps were approaching from outside Barrett's shop. We all grabbed for our swords.

"Someone must have followed you," Jonathan whispered.

The footsteps grew louder. We stared at the back door. There were at least six men by the sound of the boots on the cobblestone. We braced ourselves for the deadly fight that surely would come if these were Noble Knights.

The men walked to our door…and passed. We all breathed a sigh of relief and relaxed our swords.

"Greetings, gentlemen." A voice spoke from behind us, yet was in the same room.

I dared not turn to see the owner of the voice. It was familiar. Too familiar. The hair on my arms and neck stood straight, and I could tell that the others felt the near terror too. I did not fear the voice, but rather what the voice meant.

I must be going mad, I thought.

Slowly I turned, my eyes leading the way. Once I saw the author of those words, I stumbled back, catching myself on a center support beam. There were no words on my tongue or coherent thoughts in my mind.

Before us stood the Prince!

Some of the knights stumbled into chairs, while others grabbed something to keep themselves from falling. Two were making their way toward the back door.

I saw the scars on His body, but His strength and power seemed to be even more accentuated.

"Do not be afraid, My friends," the Prince said. "I am

not a ghost, and you are not going mad. Please sit down and let Me explain."

"M-my Lord," I stammered, "how can this be? I saw You die. I saw You hang on the tree. What trick or miracle is this?"

"A trick it is not, My dear Cedric. But miracle? Ah, yes. You see, gentlemen, My Father is not only wise and wealthy, but He also commands power that none here can comprehend. The Noble Knights will not believe, though they see Me with their own eyes. That is why My Father sent Me here to train you. You are privileged, My friends. You are part of the plan to restore His kingdom."

Slowly we came to believe that what we saw was not an apparition but truly the Prince we'd grown to love and serve. Terror and shock were eventually replaced by joy and excitement.

"Now You can help us defeat this evil Kifus and the Noble Knights, my Lord?" Rob asked.

"No, Rob. I must return to My Father's kingdom, and you will not fight Kifus and the Noble Knights."

"Then what is this all for, my Lord?" William asked.

"You must remember what I taught you and why I taught you. Your battle is with the greater foe, the Dark Knight. Do not be fooled. He also has powers that will amaze and trick many people. You must stay strong and wary. He knows I have trained you, and he will seek to destroy you before I can return. You must add to the Knights of the Prince. Be vigilant in your training, and above all, stay true to the Code. I was your example. Now you must be the example to others!"

Those same compassionate eyes—eyes that burned like fire—took each of us in.

"Why must You leave us again, my Prince?" I asked. I did not share the Prince's confidence in us.

"Cedric, your heart is strong in the Code. Trust in it and in Me. As long as you live by the Code, I will be with you. What I have taught you will not fail you. I go to prepare our kingdom across the sea for the battle that must come with the Dark Knight and his Shadow Warriors. Do not be afraid. I will come back for you."

I looked at the strong face of the Prince and found my hope again.

"Your sword is here, my Prince," I said.

I retrieved the cloth that held His glorious sword from the same chest Leinad had stored it in for so many years.

"It found me in my despair," I said and held the sword before the Prince.

He smiled and lifted it from my hands. "Do not forget, My friends. It is the Code that makes the sword worth carrying."

We all knelt before Him and then bid Him farewell.

I was lonely again, but this time I knew it would not last forever.

CHAPTER TEN

WE BUILD

 At first we worked in secret, quietly adding strength and numbers to the Knights of the Prince. But soon our confidence with the sword and our belief in the King, the Prince, and the Code drove us to recruit openly. Anyone who believed our story of the Prince and had a heart to follow the Code was welcomed and trained.

The Noble Knights hated us as they had hated the Prince. We were hunted but not defeated. The Prince had taught us well, and the Noble Knights soon realized that we were not going away. Small battles broke out across the country, but the Knights of the Prince stood strong.

Some of our men were beaten and thrown into prison, but this only solidified our resolve to accomplish our mission—to be ready for the Prince's return and to be prepared for the great battle with the Dark Knight.

"Are you ready, my brother?" I asked William.

The Code made friends of strangers and brothers of friends. William and I were now kindred spirits, not of our own doing, but because of what the Prince had taught us to believe in.

"Yes, Cedric, let's be on our way," William said. "The road is long before us, and we must make Chandril before sundown."

We set off on our journey that morning hoping to find more recruits in the neighboring city of Chandril. Along the way, we came across a man and his family journeying to our own city of Chessington. A wheel on their cart was broken, and we stopped to help. We told them of our mission and shared the story of the Prince. Their ears yearned to hear of such hope and promise.

"Please be careful in Chandril," the man said as we completed the work on his cart. "Not only is there poverty in the city, but also many of the people have become bitter and hateful. There are evil men that have great influence over the people. It is not a safe place anymore. That is why I am taking my family to Chessington."

"Find the shop owned by a man named Barrett," I said. "Tell him that William and Cedric sent you. He will help you get settled and provide protection for your family."

"Thank you for all you have done, gentlemen," the man replied. His wife smiled gratefully as they passed and proceeded on toward Chessington.

The delay caused us to arrive in Chandril at dusk. I felt the city's oppression in my spirit as we entered the outskirts. We walked up a broad street where shops were closing windows and locking doors at the end of a day's work. Our presence caught the stares of many weary faces. We stopped one fellow as he began to shut his door.

"Good sir, would you be kind enough to direct us toward the nearest inn?" William asked.

He glanced at our tunics and saw the emblem of the Prince. His face revealed his disgust.

"I have heard of your kind and your lies. Stay away from my shop!" Then he slammed the door in our faces.

A gang of six burly men across the street turned their attention to us when they heard the door slam. We walked on our way but were acutely aware of the menacing men following our every turn. They quickened their pace to gain ground. Finally we could not ignore them any longer and turned to face them.

The shops had all closed by now, and the sun was set, but there was enough residual light to see that these men were not friendly. They slowly surrounded us, each brandishing a sword on his hip. Timid faces appeared in the windows of the nearby shops and homes.

"Can we help you, gentlemen?" I asked while searching their faces for intent.

"Who are you?" the lead man asked.

"We are from Chessington and are looking for a place to stay," I said.

"I didn't ask where you were from. I recognize that mark, and it is not welcome here. You should be more careful about where you walk."

"You have allegiance to the Noble Knights then?" I asked.

"We have allegiance to no one but ourselves. Kill them

and take their money," he ordered his men.

They all drew their swords and advanced on us.

We drew our swords quickly and positioned ourselves against the wall of the shop behind us. Even if they were only average swordsmen, I knew their numbers would eventually overwhelm us.

They attacked with fury, and William and I found ourselves in a fight for our lives. Our swords collided, but there were too many of them. I injured one with a quick slice from my right, but then I caught a thrust through my left arm. The steel burned as it entered and left my flesh. I heard William gasp in pain as he caught a slice across his chest that bled profusely. He recovered and brought down his attacker with a quick thrust to his opponent's abdomen, but the leader filled his place.

Our situation was hopeless, and my thoughts turned to the Prince. Would His work here carry on effectively without us? Had we let Him down?

From within my heart came my final words to the world. I shouted for all to hear, "The King reigns—and His Son!"

Just when all seemed lost, from above our heads came the sound of deliverance. A man jumped from the roof and landed just behind the ring of attackers. From between the buildings to my left came another man who positioned himself beside the first.

The band of thieves was as shocked as we were, and the fighting momentarily stopped. The two men held brilliant swords, and they were massive men of power. Their chiseled facial features matched their muscular frames, which were partially hidden by peasant clothes. They were…Silent Warriors!

William collapsed from the loss of blood, and I moved to cover his position. The Silent Warriors advanced on the thieves without hesitation. There was no mercy. In less than a minute, four of the thieves were prone on the ground, and the remaining two managed to escape down an alleyway.

The Silent Warriors wiped their swords and sheathed them. One knelt down and lifted William with the ease of a parent lifting his child.

"I am Keef, and this is Ramon," the other knight said. "Follow me."

Keef led us to an old building near the southern part of Chandril. Once inside, Ramon laid William on a table and tore off a portion of his own tunic to dress the wound. William was still unconscious.

"Thank you for saving our lives," I said to them both. "Is William…?"

"William will live," Keef said. "Ramon will make sure of it."

It was almost an order, but Ramon nodded in agreement. I felt some relief in their confidence.

"How did you know to come to our aid?" I asked Keef.

"You spoke the words of the Prince, and your situation was desperate. Only then are we allowed to reveal ourselves."

I had forgotten what the Prince told us and felt stupid. My foolishness had nearly cost William his life.

"Is there any message from the Prince?" I asked. It had been many months since He left us to return to the King.

"We have not been home for a long time." Keef began dressing my wounded upper arm. "There is no message, but do not lose heart. Continue to build. What you tasted tonight is the work of the Dark Knight. These people do not swear allegiance to anyone. Therefore, they become his tools to work anarchy in the kingdom. When the time is right, he will sweep in and bring tyrannical rule, which the people will gladly swallow for the sake of order. The Dark Knight and his Shadow Warriors are moving, and you must be vigilant."

I watched Ramon cover William's gash with a salve from his pouch. The sweet odor of the salve filled the small room.

I turned back toward Keef. "Where did the Dark Knight come from, and why is he such a fierce enemy of the King?"

Keef finished bandaging my wound and sat down on a wooden stool. He leaned against the wall and folded one arm over his thick chest while his other hand stroked his cheek.

I saw a flood of memories pass across his thoughts. I was ready to hear a story that might make sense of this strange saga.

CHAPTER ELEVEN

ORIGINS
OF EVIL

"Ramon and I were both there," Keef began, "many, many years ago." Keef was clearly a veteran of warfare. His dark blue eyes conveyed a "serious business" attitude in all that he did. His hair was sand colored and cut short. He owned a square jaw that matched his determination. His broad neck, shoulders, and arms revealed tremendous strength, and his hands dwarfed my own.

Yes, Keef would make a most formidable foe. I was glad to be on the same side.

Ramon finished dressing William's wound and joined us on another stool. Ramon was just as large as Keef with slightly darker skin and hair. He was a man of action and very few words.

Keef continued. "In our kingdom across the sea, life was peaceful, and the Dark Knight was not always our enemy. In fact, he was the head of the Silent Warriors. There were nearly five thousand of us. We followed his orders without question. He proved himself to be the best of the best and won favor with the King. His given name is Lucius. Next to the King and His Son, no one had more authority or power than Lucius."

"I don't understand," I said. "What happened to make Lucius the King's archenemy?"

Keef hesitated as he pondered his memories. "I'm not sure, Cedric. You have lived with the Prince and know that there is only kindness and compassion in His heart. I believe the only reason Lucius eventually turned on the Prince was pure jealousy. I am sure that his pride in his own ability, and pride in his power, ultimately led to his downfall.

"I first noticed it during our drills. One day the Prince came to check on us as Lucius led us through the training. When the Prince approached, Lucius bowed, but not in heart. I sensed the slightest hint of contempt. And when the Prince left us, Lucius watched Him carefully; his thoughts were clearly elsewhere. I was not the only knight that noticed. Most of us questioned our own judgment, yet some seemed interested in Lucius's newfound arrogance.

"As the weeks wore on, Lucius grew more and more rebellious in front of the knights, and yet he hid it from the Prince and the King. One of the knights approached him about his attitude. Lucius pulled him aside and spoke but a few brief words to that knight. We saw fear on the knight's face, and he was silent from then on. None of us dared challenge Lucius, for none could defeat him.

"However, a commander's heart is not his own. I felt the disdain and rebellious attitudes filtering down the ranks. Many of the knights were more loyal to Lucius than to the King and the Prince. Risking our lives at the hand of Lucius, Ramon and I decided to take the matter to the Prince."

William moaned on the table as he stirred. Ramon and I walked over to check on him, but he fell back asleep.

As I returned to my stool to hear the rest of Keef's story, I became acutely aware of my hunger. We had not eaten since arriving in Chandril, and all the activity had eliminated any opportunity to eat. I reached for the provisions we had brought for the journey and offered some to the Silent Warriors. They accepted graciously, and while they ate, I waited patiently for the rest of Keef's story, pondering all that he had told me already. Keef finished his food and drank heavily from his water flask. He leaned back on his stool and continued.

"Ramon and I agreed to approach the King's palace at night so as not to draw attention to ourselves. Even at night, the palace is more glorious than anything else I have ever seen. You and William will see it one day, Cedric. All of the Knights of the Prince will see it.

"As we came to the palace, four other knights intercepted us. We greeted them and tried to pass on nonchalantly, but they would not give way. It was only then that I realized just how serious the situation had become. We were men sworn to the King. We trained and fought side by side and even ate our meals together. We wore the same emblem.

"But these four had changed their allegiance. The realization of their actions shocked me. We tried to appeal to their sworn loyalty, but it was clear they had crossed the line.

They threatened to kill us if we would not join them. For the first time in the history of the King's kingdom, two swords of the Silent Warriors met as enemies. A rebellion was born.

"We fought defensively at first, still not wanting to believe what was happening. But when they drew first blood on Ramon, we knew there was no turning back."

Ramon lifted the portion of his tunic that remained, after having used part of it for William's bandage, and revealed a deep scar that crossed his chest.

Keef continued. "Ramon quickly recovered and slew his attacker. I injured a second to make the fight even, but our skirmish brought attention, and three more knights came to join the fight. I recognized them and guessed them to be loyal to Lucius. I was right. Our situation was grave. We fought back-to-back to provide as much protection for each other as possible, but we could not last long."

Keef's eyes narrowed and his brows furrowed. I sympathized with him, having just escaped our own deaths by a very narrow margin.

"I was never so glad to see the Prince ride up on His white stallion as I was that night. The five traitorous knights ran to the shadows and disappeared. Their boldness temporarily faded in the presence of the Prince. We explained our understanding of the situation to the Prince as we walked with Him to the palace.

"'Come with Me to the King,' the Prince said. Micalem, second in command under Lucius and a brilliant knight as well as an outstanding warrior, joined us inside the palace. His face revealed his sorrow at the news of the rebellion.

"The three of us and the Prince entered the throne room and approached the King. We knelt before His Majesty, and He bid us to rise. 'It has happened, Father,' the Prince said. 'Yes, as I feared it would,' the King said. 'Gather the Silent Warriors who are loyal and prepare for war, My Son.' 'As you wish, Father,' the Prince said.

"We bowed and left the King. The Prince took us to another chamber. 'Micalem,' he said, 'you are now in command of the Silent Warriors. Stay with Me to plan our next move. Keef and Ramon, gather those you know to be loyal and brief them on the situation. Then spread out and gather all other loyal knights. Gentlemen, there is no war more deadly or devastating than a war from within. Be careful.'

"We turned to leave. 'Keef, Ramon,' the Prince said, 'well done!' 'Well done' was all He said, and yet it was all I needed to take on an army. When we go back home, those are the words I hope to hear again.

"We gathered our men through the night, and by morning the lines were drawn. Lucius had claimed over fifteen hundred knights. Some of our finest warriors had sided with him—men such as Envor, Hatlin, and Luskan. Knights we had respected and admired were now our enemies. I still don't understand how Lucius convinced them to turn against the King!

"The war was fierce, but we outnumbered them two to one. Their only option was to flee the kingdom or be destroyed. And that, Sir Cedric, is why this land is in peril. The Dark Knight brought his Shadow Warriors, as they became known, to this kingdom. Although this land is the

King's, the Dark Knight is determined to rule it. And if he can't rule it, he will destroy it. You may never have seen the Dark Knight, but you can be sure he is here. Even the Silent Warriors fear his fight, for he is powerful and merciless. Only the Prince Himself is able to overcome him."

"But why did the Prince come here disguised as a peasant?" I said. "Why not just bring an entire army and retake the kingdom?"

"Because He doesn't want just a kingdom, Cedric," Keef said. "He wants a kingdom of people with hearts that love and serve willingly. People like you. He wants people who honestly desire to follow the Code. A full-scale assault on this land would destroy that. The King loves these people, and He has provided a way for them to live."

"The Prince made a way, didn't He?" I asked.

"That's right. I remember the day when the King told us of His plan to save this land. We could not believe He would jeopardize His own Son to save this kingdom. At first we thought it was foolish, but soon we realized it was pure love—love for the people. The Prince understood, and we knew He was the only one capable of being successful.

"We were all at the palace to bid Him farewell. He came from the inner court, and we all knelt before Him. Thousands of knights in shining armor knelt before the Prince, who was dressed in dirty rags. But those clothes couldn't hide the splendor of His character, as you saw."

"Yes, Keef," I said. "There was something about that man!"

"We rose and saluted the Prince with drawn swords as He passed between our lines. When He neared the gates, the King walked to His Son and embraced Him. I saw a tear fall from the King's cheek and moisten the beautiful stones at their feet. Then He left. We tried to provide an escort, but He refused. He took no weapon, not even a sword. He said He would live as the people do for a time, and He limited our mission while He was here."

Keef's story provided many answers, but there was still one question to ask. "The Dark Knight must have known that the Prince was in the kingdom," I said, finding affirmation in a nod from Keef. "Why didn't the Dark Knight attempt to kill the Prince before He had a chance to train and to build up our forces?"

Keef leaned forward, rested his left elbow on his knee, and placed his right hand on the other knee. His eyes sparkled as though he was anxious to answer.

"He did, Cedric! Do you remember the last time you and William visited Leinad?"

"Yes, it was just a few days before the Prince revealed Himself as the King's Son in the square."

"That's right," Keef said. "Later that day, the Prince, Ramon, and I visited Leinad too. He had kept the sword of the Prince for years, waiting for the day to give it to Him. That was the day—the day when the 'one who is worthy' would carry the sword and deliver the people…deliver the kingdom!

"When we entered his home, Leinad came and stood before the Prince. He looked into the eyes of the King's Son, then reached forth and placed his hand on the Prince's chest. I could see the burden of fifty years leave his face. 'Now I rest, for the mighty arm of the King has arrived!'

Leinad said, and he knelt before the Prince. 'You are a true and faithful knight, Sir Leinad,' the Prince said. He helped Leinad to his feet. 'Please bring the chest,' Leinad asked Ramon and me.

"We retrieved the old wooden chest from the corner, placed it at Leinad's feet, and opened it for him. He carefully unfolded the cloth that was wrapped about the sword and reverently lifted it to the Prince. 'Only one is worthy,' Leinad said as the Prince placed His hand about the hilt of the beautiful sword. The Prince raised the sword before Him and proclaimed, 'Now is the time. Let it begin!'

"At the command of the Prince, two other Silent Warriors escorted Leinad to a ship that awaited to take him to the kingdom across the sea. His mission was complete, and the King had called him home.

"From Leinad's home, we followed the Prince deep into the country on horseback. The Dark Knight knew that he would rule this kingdom forever if he could destroy the Prince. Thus…the challenge."

Keef paused, gathering details in his mind.

"What was the challenge?" I asked, too impatient to wait for him to continue on his own.

After another moment of thoughtful silence, Keef continued. "The Dark Knight challenged the Prince to a single duel, hoping to kill the Prince and end His mission before it began. The Prince accepted because He knew it was His final preparation for the monumental task before Him. Defeating the Dark Knight would confirm Him as the only true authority in Arrethtrae.

"On the crest of a hill near the base of the Northern

Mountains, we joined with two hundred mounted Silent Warriors. Apprehension hung in the air. Across a span of rugged terrain, many of the Dark Knight's Shadow Warriors lined the horizon. The Prince rode before our solemn line. 'This is neither the time nor the place for battle,' He said for all to hear. 'This fight is for Me alone!'

"The Prince rode to meet Lucius midway. As the distance between the champion of darkness and the champion of light closed, a silence fell upon the countryside. Even the birds stopped their song. It was as though nature itself recognized the potential peril of the land. Dark clouds had rolled in and obscured the sun, but now the air was silent—a calm before the storm. I remember thinking how ironic it was that the fate of all the people of Arrethtrae would ride on the outcome of this single fight, and they were completely ignorant of its happening.

"With only a few strides between them, Lucius and the Prince dismounted and drew their swords. The ultimate battle between the two best swordsmen that ever lived was about to begin. Hatred versus love. Bondage versus freedom. The Dark Knight versus the Prince. The future of Arrethtrae was unfolding at this very moment.

"They slowly circled each other at a safe distance, calculating and planning their strategies, it appeared—feeling the terrain, anticipating strengths, looking for weaknesses. The silence of the countryside gave way to an eerie, low growl that built in strength and emanated from the unified voices of the Shadow Warriors. It was the taunting war cry of a vicious enemy, heightened by the distant thunder of storm clouds.

"Micalem was first to respond. 'Honor…glory…power… the Prince!' he shouted. 'Honor…glory…power…the Prince!' The chant flowed down our line until the words resonated off the hillsides and mixed with the opposing growl in a bizarre and unnatural song. The rhythm and intensity increased with the roar and flash of lightning—all in anticipation of the first strike.

"Lucius and the Prince simultaneously positioned themselves and readied their swords. Lucius struck first, and both lines of warriors yielded to silent observation as the fight ensued. Lucius engaged with a quick combination, and the Prince met each stroke with precision.

"I realized that my heart was pounding and my muscles were taut. I tried to relax, but could not; too much was at stake. The fight quickly developed into a ferocious volley of cuts, slices, and thrusts. The steel of their blades screamed through the air unceasingly. Two unyielding masters were in a battle to the death. Lucius attacked with the speed of a viper, and the Prince countered with the power of a lion."

Keef leaned back and drew in a deep breath. "I am a warrior well acquainted with battle, Cedric. But I must admit that the intensity of that duel between Lucius and the Prince made it frightening to watch."

I glanced at Ramon. His eyes were shut, and a nearly imperceptible nod affirmed Keef's feeling of unease during the fight.

"At one point in the fight, Lucius aggressively advanced with a quick series of combinations that caused the Prince to move back. His foot caught on a stone behind Him, and He fell. Lucius instantly brought down a powerful vertical cut on the Prince. Flat on His back, and with no time or place to move, the Prince executed a quick parry that deflected Lucius's blade. The sword tore into the ground to the left of the Prince's shoulder.

"The Prince rolled to the right and onto His knees, but the maneuver momentarily exposed His back to the enemy. Anticipating Lucius's next move, the Prince swiftly locked His sword above His head and caught Lucius's next vertical cut. The Prince rotated on one knee and exploded a horizontal slice that moved at blinding speed full circle around to Lucius. Lucius jumped back as the tip of the Prince's sword grazed his chest. This gave the Prince enough time to recover and reestablish His position. I heard Lucius curse over his lost opportunity.

"The thunderstorm was now upon us, and day turned to night. The lightning flashed from cloud to cloud, and the ground shook with the roar of thunder. Our horses pawed the ground nervously.

"Lucius advanced again. His fight teetered on the edge of recklessness—he was taking risks he had not taken in the beginning. He appeared to be obsessed with destroying the Prince and willing to risk injury to himself to do it. But the Prince stood firm, and there was no breach in His defense. Lucius's ferocity was wearing him down, and the fight began to tilt. The Prince advanced with such power and speed that Lucius found himself in retreat. The sky began to unload its burden of water in a steady rain that soaked my clothes instantly.

"Lucius attempted a more offensive posture, but the Prince was now in control, and I'm sure Lucius knew it.

The Prince paused and stared at His archenemy. The scowl on Lucius's face revealed his hatred for this enemy and also, I think, his understanding that the future of Arrethtrae belonged to the Prince!

"The Prince advanced with combinations and maneuvers I had never seen before. His dominance over Lucius was unbelievable! It was time for the end, and the Prince brought forth a sequence of cuts that nearly paralyzed Lucius. One massive blow caused Lucius to lose his balance and his sword. The grisly weapon of the Dark Knight was finally still, and Lucius lay prone before the Prince.

"The entire line of Silent Warriors cheered in victory. The Prince glared at this enemy of two kingdoms and spoke. 'My Father loved you, and you spurned His love. He has postponed your judgment for now. Your final destruction is yet before you, but it is a certainty!'

"The Prince withdrew and mounted His stallion. We rode to a distant camp. He was tired, and we guarded Him while He ate and slept.

"Two days later you saw Him in the square. From that day on, our involvement in His mission has been extremely limited. It was hard not to be by His side. When they took Him to the tree, a thousand Silent Warriors were ready to wipe out the entire city. But He forbade us. He did it for you, Cedric. He did it for all the people who will follow Him."

My eyes filled with tears again as I remembered that day in the square. How could anyone care that much for me?

There was a long silence before Ramon spoke. "It is time to leave, Keef."

"Yes, Ramon, I suppose you are right. Take care, Cedric.

And remember, the story did not end at the tree. For you and your people, that is where the story begins."

"Thank you, Keef," I said. "Thank you, Ramon. I will not forget you. May we meet again someday!"

"We will, Cedric," Keef said. "We will!"

And with that, they donned their crude cloaks again and entered the streets. As the door closed, William stirred and awoke.

"Lie still, brother," I said.

"Where are we, Cedric?" William asked. "I thought we were going to die. What happened?"

I chuckled. "I don't think you're going to believe me, but I'll give it a try anyway."

CHAPTER TWELVE

NIGHT OF KNIGHTS

 The Knights of the Prince grew tremendously in numbers, and the anarchy of the kingdom seemed to match our pace. The kingdom of Arrethtrae was on the verge of self-destruction, like a volcano ready to erupt. We built and strengthened, but the Dark Knight countered with discord and chaos.

We sent recruiters for the Prince to every city in the kingdom. We worked hard for years, and eventually nearly everyone—men, women, and children—heard the story of the Prince and was given an opportunity to join us. It was during these years that many valiant men and women rose up to fulfill the mission of the Prince.

Our beloved city of Chessington seemed to be the Dark Knight's focus. We began seeing more and more of the Shadow Warriors. They were disguised as commoners, but we could tell they were much more than that.

The Noble Knights faded into history and either gave

way or were absorbed into a new form of government. The city chose a strong man by the name of Alexander Histen as its governor. *Strong* is a broad description of Governor Histen. It applies to his physical strength as well as his political might. His charisma seemed to magnetize the people to his cause.

I did not like him nor was I fooled by his sweet rhetoric. As chaos increased, so did his control over the people. It was "necessary," so Governor Histen said, "to maintain security and peace in the city." He convinced the people it was for their own good. The desperate citizens swallowed it all, for they had no choice.

In the back of my mind, I wondered how much of the chaos was generated by Histen himself. It was just as Keef had told me.

Over the next year, Alexander Histen widened his sphere of influence to include most of the surrounding cities and villages. Histen scoffed at our story of the return of the Prince and denied altogether the King's authority in the land. He labeled us as haters of peace and harmony, the very antithesis of what we were. His propaganda worked, and our mission became much more difficult. Serious persecution returned. Many of the Knights of the Prince were beaten and imprisoned for the crime of causing a disturbance in the city. My own scars testify to such atrocities.

In spite of this, we still found people hungry for hope. They yearned for truth and peace with freedom as a companion, for the peace they tasted now was falsely induced under tyrannical rule.

Eventually, Histen changed his title to Governor Supreme.

It was clear to us that he cared for only one thing—total control of the entire kingdom.

During these difficult times, our belief in the Code is what kept us together.

"How long will this go on, Cedric?" William asked as we walked toward the meeting place.

Barrett's shop had been discovered and burned some time ago. We found a safer place for him and his family on the outskirts of the city, but our new meeting place was still in the heart of the city.

"It does seem nearly impossible to continue, doesn't it," I said. "It's been so long since the Prince left us, and yet I know He will be true to His word and deliver us from this bondage."

The moonlight lit our path, and we moved carefully down the streets and alleys, ever vigilant to watch all sides.

"Ironic, isn't it?" William said quietly. "When we first met the Prince, we felt we were in bondage to poverty, but now we know what true bondage is. I don't see any end to Histen's desire for power and control of the people."

We turned onto another alley and began walking down it.

"Nor do I, Will—"

I stopped midsentence, and we both took cover in the shadows. Other men occupied the alley already. We were not seen, for they too were deep in conversation, and they were walking our way.

They paused some fifty feet away. Both men were broad and tall. I had never seen either one before, but I recognized their posture. Fear began to grip my heart, and I fought to maintain control of it. Though they were dressed in common clothes, I knew they were either Silent Warriors or Shadow Warriors.

William and I froze in the shadows and strained to hear their conversation. They spoke softly, but their deep voices carried far enough for us to hear.

"—nearly complete with his preparation plans in the North," one of them said.

"How is Kelson doing in the south? We must be ready in all quadrants or the mission will be delayed. Time is short," the other one said.

"He is nearly ready, but I must tell you—"

Crash!

A door beside the two figures burst open, and a huge, menacing man lunged toward the two figures with sword drawn. Across the alley, two more monstrous men flew toward the same two figures, each flashing a wicked looking sword.

In the blink of an eye, the two figures threw back their cloaks and drew their swords. Back-to-back, they faced their enemies. They had the look of serious determination, but not the look of hate that was on the faces of their three attackers

The swords flew at blinding speed. We heard a thunderous and continuous clash of steel upon steel. I had seen the skill of a Silent Warrior against mere men, and I had fought against a Shadow Warrior firsthand, but never before had I seen two such formidable forces meet face-to-face. The fight raged on in a flurry of slices, cuts, and thrusts—a precise picture of good versus evil.

"William," I whispered, "we must help them!"

"I am ready," he said.

Though my stomach rose to my throat, we drew our swords and ran toward the battle.

"For the Prince!" William shouted.

At those words, one of the Shadow Warriors left his fight and lunged toward us. Anger burned in his eyes.

William and I traded offensive and defensive posturing to keep the Shadow Warrior distracted. Our past encounters with the Shadow Warriors had taught us a great deal, and we had grown in strength, skill, and experience. William defended against a combination, and I saw an opportunity, which I took.

The Shadow Warrior screamed a curse at me as my sword passed under his left arm and separated the flesh beneath his ribs. He charged me with a full-force blow that sent me stumbling. He seized the momentary break in our fight to escape between two buildings, clutching his side as he went.

We moved toward the other fight, but these Shadow Warriors also took flight. All of us scanned the area for further threat, but found none.

After a moment of silence, interrupted only by heavy breathing, we sheathed our swords.

"Thank you for your help," one of the Silent Warriors said. "Normally we avoid such confrontations, but lately it has not been possible. Their presence here is growing quickly."

"Yes, we've noticed as well," I said. "What does it mean?"

He searched my face with narrow eyes. "You are Cedric?"

"I am. And this is William."

"We must go. Time is short—very short. Tell your people to be ready!"

He nodded to his companion toward one side of the alley, and together they left us quickly and quietly.

"Be ready for what?" I asked, but there was no one to answer.

CHAPTER THIRTEEN

CHANGE
OF HEART

 Over the next three days, we spread the message from the Silent Warrior to the Knights of the Prince: "Be ready!"

Of course, everyone repeated my statement with a question: "Be ready for what?" But before we could discover the answer, the kingdom of Arrethtrae saw the dawn of total oppression.

I AWOKE TO A MORNING that was bright and cool, yet I felt a heavy darkness descend like a thick fog. I attributed it to a restless night's sleep and tried to shake it off as I washed my face in cool water, but it lingered.

Rob, William, and I journeyed to northern Chessington to organize a mission that would send us beyond our region. The city of Drisdol was in desperate need of supplies. Those who pledged allegiance to the Prince were plundered daily by Histen's men. Though we suffered similar persecution in Chessington, our city was larger and afforded greater protection and supplies.

For several streets, we walked in vigilant silence. William spoke first. "There is evil in the city today."

"I feel it too." Rob's ever-present grin was absent. "We've done all we can to recruit people for the Prince. Our numbers are great, but Histen's oppression and control increase with each passing day. How long must we carry on? Why must we carry on?"

I felt Rob's despair and was also growing weary of the fight. Our brothers and sisters were persecuted continuously. Histen wanted us out of his way, and I knew that persecution would soon turn to killing. Yet the Prince was—

"Get your grimy paws off my fruit, you filthy li'l mutt."

The shouts of a produce shop owner interrupted my thoughts. A young boy scampered over a barrel and knocked down the shop owner's fruit and vegetable stand. The boy ran across the street with a stolen apple in hand. We winced at the string of cursing that followed. The shop owner's face was red with rage, and he emphasized each curse with a clenched fist.

The curses eventually subsided until he turned to see his produce scattered on the walk and the street.

"May we help you, sir?" I asked as politely as possible, hoping to soothe his anger a bit.

The man was barrel-chested with stocky legs to match. He looked middle-aged, and his curly dark hair was laced with wisps of gray. He glanced our way, but his countenance had not changed. The anger in his face seemed to be a steady companion.

"You stay away from my food," he bellowed. "I'm no fool to trust the likes of you nor any other thief in this city."

He yelled over his shoulder toward the shop door. "Cassy! Get out here an' clean this mess up, right now!"

Within seconds, a woman who appeared to be his wife emerged. I could see her beauty beneath the lines of strife and bruises of abuse on her face. She did not look up at us but quickly moved toward the spill, taking care not to get too close to her husband. His lingering anger was still evident. He raised his hand to strike and vent his frustration as she passed.

"I would advise you not to do that, sir," William said as we stepped forward.

The man turned to look at us. "I will do as I please, and you will stay out of my business!"

It was enough distraction for his wife to pass by beyond his reach. The moment passed, and he cursed at us as he turned to right his produce stand.

Rob's face displayed the anger we all felt as we stepped into the street to pass this shop of despair. A few steps brought us to the man's wife, and we knelt to help her fill a basket.

"Please—no!" came a soft plea from her weathered lips. "Just leave now or he will hurt me more."

The man was kneeling and reaching for a broken table leg near the base of his shop's front wall when he glanced up to see us giving aid to his wife. "You get your—aaah!"

His scream seemed the result of searing pain. He stood

up to reveal a fire asp coiled around his forearm.

The fire asp is not only the deadliest snake in the kingdom, but its effects on its victim are horrific. The poison is quick, and death is certain once it reaches the brain. Its length is a little longer than a man's foot, and its breadth is no bigger around than a finger. It is brown in color, making it difficult to see until it strikes, when the skin of the asp changes to a fiery red. It is aggressive and bites only once. It then dies with its victim.

The initial sensation around the bite is a torturous burning and swelling that spreads with the poison until searing pain permeates the entire body. As the poison enters the brain, the overwhelming pain drives the victim into madness. Death follows within moments of the initial bite.

The shop owner continued to scream as he clutched his right arm with his left hand. Panic was evident on his face.

"William! Rob! Quick—come with me," I shouted. We ran to the man and sat him on the ground. "William, remove the asp with your knife. Rob, give him something to bite on and hold his arm steady!"

The man's wife slowly stood up and backed into the shop. Her mouth was open and shock was on her face.

"Stay as calm as you can, sir. The slower your heart beats, the better chance we have of saving your life," I said as gently as possible.

My grandfather had once saved his brother from the poisonous bite of a fire asp, but I knew the odds were slim. I had never heard of any other victim living through the ordeal.

I secured a leather strap around the man's upper arm

and tightened it until no blood could flow in either direction. William finished removing the asp, and it lay limp and lifeless on the walk. The swelling was already spreading to the man's hand and to his upper arm. So was the pain. His legs shook violently, and the cloth between his teeth only slightly muffled his screams.

"William, quickly make some mud from the alley and bring it here," I said.

I unsheathed my knife and opened a vein above and below the bite to spill the contaminated blood. I massaged his arm toward the cuts to empty the veins. I knew he might lose his arm, but it was his only hope. William returned with the mud.

"We must prick his arm in multiple places before we apply the mud," I told William.

Rob was occupied holding down the man's other arm. I glanced at the man's shoulder to see if the poison had spread beyond my leather strap and was slightly relieved to see no evidence of swelling there. The small cuts we gave him hardly bled—a good sign too. We quickly encased his entire arm in thick, cool mud to draw the poison out.

"What next, Cedric?" William asked.

"Now we wait, gentlemen," I said. "We will know in a moment if we are successful. I must loosen the strap and return blood to his arm, or he will lose it. But if I do this before the mud has drawn out the poison, it will spread, and he will die."

I looked for his wife, but she was gone. If we were successful, I wondered if I had condemned her to a slower, more painful death than her husband was facing. During

such times, there is little time to think, only time to re
What would the Prince do next? I wondered.

Moments passed. The man was still breathing and h
not gone mad. The mud was drying, and the pain seeme
to ease.

I slowly loosened the leather strap and watched for the
swelling to spread. The mud began to turn red from the
new flow of blood to the cuts we had made in his arm.

The swelling seemed to be contained, so we peeled the
mud off. After washing his arm with clean water, we
applied a clean bandage. Although his arm was twice its
normal size, enough time had passed to know that he was
not going to die.

He wiped away the tears that ran down his face. We
gave him some water to drink and leaned him against the
front of his shop.

"Who are you?" he whispered.

"I am Cedric. This is William and Rob. We are Knights
of the Prince."

He breathed deeply and closed his eyes.

"Thank you. Thank you," came a weak but sincere
reply. "I do not know why anyone would bother to save the
likes of me. Even my wife is gone, and I do not blame her."

"We have seen the compassion of the Prince and know
that every man is worth saving," William said.

"Will you listen to our story of His love for the kingdom
and for you?" Rob asked.

"I am anxious to hear it, for I don't even know what
kindness and love are," the man said. "I have never seen
nor felt them…until today."

...r name, sir?" I asked.

...Derek. Please, tell me of this man you call

...eager to hear our story of the King's great love
...ple—a love so great that He sent His Son to teach
...ultimately, to die for us. We told of the Prince's
...ious reappearance and of His promise to take us to
...kingdom where there is no hunger or despair.

Each word of our story began to soften Derek's heart. A
...art as hard as granite was slowly transformed to a heart
...eady to give and receive compassion. The story of the
Prince does that to men. It breaks them down, removes the
rubble, and builds a castle where there once was a prison.

Derek wiped more tears from his eyes. This time they
were tears of repentance and joy.

"Please come to my house for a meal," Derek pleaded.
"I want you to meet my family."

We traveled one street to the east of his shop and found
ourselves approaching the door of his home. Two small,
frightened faces peered out the window as we approached.
When we entered his home, the children did not run to greet
their father. They each darted to a corner to hide behind a
piece of furniture. His wife, Cassy, was shocked that he
was alive, and she slowly moved to the back of the room.

Derek walked slowly toward his wife. She looked like a
cornered mouse, too afraid to move. I thought she might
collapse from her fear.

The little boy and girl seemed to know what was coming and buried their heads in their knees, covering their
ears with little hands.

"Cassy," Derek said in a hushed, quavering voice. Tears rushed to his eyes once again and flowed down his cheeks. "I am so very sorry." He dropped to his knees before his wife. His large shoulders heaved with each sob. "How can you ever forgive me?" His hand reached to gently touch the hem of her tattered skirt.

Cassy looked at Derek's bowed head for a moment, perhaps waiting for this horrible trick to end. She looked at her children and then at us.

I smiled and nodded to affirm the reality of Derek's transformed heart.

She slowly moved her calloused hand to Derek's head. It was a gesture of forgiveness, though she could not yet speak the words. Her eyes welled up with tears, and I knew her heart wanted to believe the unbelievable. How could years of abuse be stripped away in an afternoon? It was an emotional reconciliation for everyone.

The children were surprised at the silence and stole a peek to see their father humbled on the floor before their mother.

Derek looked up and beckoned for his children. Slowly they left their cover and cautiously approached Derek. The girl placed a protective arm around her little brother.

"Daddy, please don't hurt us anymore," said the tender little voice of the girl. Derek carefully leaned forward to span the remaining distance between him and his children. He gently brought them into his arms, and his weeping deepened.

"I promise I will never hurt you or your mother ever again," he said. "I love you, children."

Their little arms wrapped around his neck, and I was certain it was the first time they had felt their daddy's love.

Derek slowly stood and let Cassy look at his moist face. Her eyes were full and her lip quivered as she yielded her heart to the truth that Derek was a new man.

"I love you, Cassy. I hope there's room left in your heart to love me...even just a little." Derek's arms encircled her with the morning embrace of love.

"Oh, Derek!" Cassy said, and she melted into his embrace.

I leaned toward Rob. "This is why we must carry on, my brother!"

CHAPTER FOURTEEN

AGE OF DARKNESS

 During the meal with Derek and his family, we shared the story of the Prince with Cassy and the children. They too understood, believed, and were born into a new life of hope. The spilled blood of the Prince caused love and compassion to flourish where there once was a desert. This family was transformed by His story, and I knew they would never be the same.

We left their home and traveled on to our destination in northern Chessington. Our mutual joy in sharing compassion with a family had been uplifting but brief.

We passed a variety of shops and homes along the way. On every corner a message was posted, and the usual bustle of activity on the streets paused as small assemblies gathered to read what had been posted. The dust of the streets settled while all of Arrethtrae held its breath. We joined the crowd at one street corner and read the following:

Attention Citizens of Arrethtrae!

Governor Supreme Alexander Histen is hereby appointed King of Arrethtrae. All people will swear allegiance to King Alexander Histen and acknowledge his authority over all subjects by complying with the following proclamation:

1. All subjects will bow in the presence of King Alexander Histen.

2. All subjects will pay a permit fee to the King in exchange for the privilege of buying and selling goods in the kingdom of Arrethtrae. Upon the purchase of this permit, the King's insignia will be imprinted upon the subject's right hand. Any subject attempting to buy or sell goods without the imprint of the King will be punished!

3. No subject will acknowledge the existence of any authority other than King Alexander Histen. Violation of this order is punishable by death!

4. No subject is allowed to carry a sword without explicit approval of the King. All swords will be collected within the next two days.

5. No subject is allowed to travel beyond the limits of the city they reside in without proper authorization from the King.

6. No subject is allowed to travel at night without proper authorization from the King.

Any subject who fails to comply with all points of this proclamation will be immediately punished.

All Hail King Alexander Histen!

We stood in silence as the severity of this edict settled into our minds. It was the beginning of a new age of darkness. *What will happen to the Knights of the Prince?* I wondered.

"Well, gentlemen, life has just become very, very hard," William said.

"Yes, it has," I said. "But what better time than now to spread the words of the Prince? The people will feel the iron hand of Histen and know bondage as they have never known it before. He is trying to strip the people of all hope, but we will give it to them. We will find a way to carry on. The Prince expects no less from us. Let us unite in an inseparable bond of brotherhood and fulfill our duty to the Code, the Prince, and the true King of Arrethtrae!"

I placed my hands on the shoulders of William and Rob. I was confident that they too knew we must press on. Too much was at stake for us to lose hope and give up.

"Let us not forget the promise of the Prince. He will return," I said, hoping to encourage them as well as myself.

William's jaw tightened in determination, and Rob nodded as we vowed to persevere no matter the cost.

The grain of our vow was quickly tested. Four of Histen's men were collecting a "fee" from a shop owner across the street. This was a normal practice since Histen had come to power, but the new proclamation gave his men renewed arrogance.

"In addition to our fee, King Histen requires your daughter to come and serve in his palace," we heard the lead henchman say.

He was the largest of the four and wore a black beard cut close to his skin. His thick chest and dark eyes made him formidable. His three cohorts did not look as threatening, though sometimes looks are misleading. They sneered and obviously enjoyed the anguish they were about to cause this poor man and his daughter.

William, Rob, and I began to walk across the street toward the skirmish.

"I have paid you faithfully for over a year," the man said. "I have even sworn allegiance to King Histen. My wife has died, and my daughter is all that is important to me. You ask too much! I will not hand over my daughter to King Histen or to anyone else!"

"Then we will take her by force. Step aside!"

I heard a panicked scream from within the shop as the owner tried to stop the brutes from entering.

"Leave him alone!" I shouted.

Rob and William positioned themselves on my left and right, a few yards in front of the shop. The three of us were no longer amateur swordsmen. Over the past few years, we had honed our skills and fought many enemies. If I must fight a battle, I prefer William and Rob at my side. They are veterans and men of honor—men that I can trust.

The four men turned to see what insolent fool dared to challenge them. The leader gazed harshly at us.

"Who dares challenge my authority and interfere in the King's business?" The man threatened more than he asked.

"No one you need be concerned with…as long as you leave the man and his daughter alone," William said.

"You are in violation of the King's proclamation. Hand over your swords immediately or you will be severely punished," the leader said.

"We will give our swords to you, but you will not enjoy the manner in which they come," Rob said as his hand came to rest on the hilt of his sword.

The leader became enraged at our defiance and drew his sword from his scabbard. Within seconds, six more swords slid from scabbards, filling the air with a brief harmony of sliding steel on steel. The leader spoke in hushed tones to one of his men, and the man withdrew slightly from the impending fight. Three of them charged, and we readied ourselves for the assault. The bearded leader came for me.

I was challenged by my foe, as was William by his, but Rob gained the upper hand on his opponent quickly. He maneuvered him off to the left and away from the shop's door. The owner disappeared within, presumably to protect his daughter. From the corner of my eye, I saw the fourth man heading east toward Histen's palace.

A strong blow came from my left. I blocked it with the flat of my sword and countered with a slice across the middle that grazed my enemy's right shoulder. He cursed but was not seriously injured, and he renewed his fight with vehemence. I saw Rob parry a weak cut and counter with a quick thrust that put his opponent down.

"Rob," I called, "get the man and his daughter south to Barrett. I fear reinforcements are coming, so you'll have to move fast. We'll meet up with you there."

Rob entered the shop, and I turned my full attention to my opponent. William gained the upper hand, and his foe backed off and ran east. The bearded leader withdrew also. Down the street from the east, I saw a band of men coming speedily.

"You will pay for your treason with your lives!" the leader screamed.

We ran into the shop and locked the door, then exited through a back door into an alleyway. I saw Rob and his new companions at a distance to the south, but they were still vulnerable.

"William, we must stall Histen's men. We have to buy Rob enough time to get the man and his daughter to safety," I said.

The shouts of men were getting closer with each passing moment. We ran through another shop and onto a street parallel to the street on which the fight had begun. We ran north one street, then west. Histen's men followed as we had hoped, but we kept them at a safe distance. Finally, we lost our pursuers and found refuge in a small, unoccupied hut off the main streets.

William and I rested, waiting for Histen's men to abandon their search. It was some time before we ventured out again.

"I hope Rob was successful," William said.

"Many hours have passed—ample time for them to reach safety," I said. "Let's take the back way out into the alley and start making our way home."

"I'm more than ready to go home, my friend," William said.

We slowly entered the alley, keeping a careful watch on

the street just to the left of us. At last, there was no sign of a search, and we were relieved. The alley felt more secure than the street we were about to enter—or so I thought.

Behind us, a subdued, evil-sounding chuckle broke my false hopes of seclusion. As we turned, the chuckle became a pompous, roaring laugh. Chills traveled up my spine.

It was Alexander Histen himself! He was mounted on a black stallion, which snorted and flared its nostrils. On each side of Histen stood four of the largest warriors I had ever seen. All four were darkly dressed, with leather straps crossing their chests. Each stood a full head taller than William or I. Obvious veterans of sword fighting, each owned a variety of scars. Their muscular frames alone were forbidding, but the massive swords they carried finished the picture of undaunted destruction these men were clearly capable of. We had faced similar foes before—these were Shadow Warriors.

Their brazen appearance with Histen told me one thing: The Dark Knight was near! Surely this was the age of darkness the Prince had spoken of. I glanced at William and knew he felt the same fear I was fighting.

The four Shadow Warriors surrounded us. We stepped back toward the rock wall on the side of the alley. I thought that to draw our swords would mean quick and certain death.

Histen spoke in a thick, condescending tone. "So this is Sir William and Sir Cedric of Chessington."

Although I had never seen Histen up close, he seemed as large as the Shadow Warriors. I was sure this perception was because he was mounted.

"Your little escapades around the kingdom are over!" he said as he dismounted the stallion.

As he approached, he seemed to grow with each stride until I realized that Alexander Histen stood shoulder to shoulder with the Shadow Warriors. Unlike them, however, his face and exposed skin were free from any scars. His hair was jet-black and cut short. His facial features were sharp, and his eyes were deep, dark, and penetrating. It was clear he was the only author of commands when present.

"I am King of Arrethtrae. I will show mercy and allow you one chance to swear allegiance to me," Histen said.

In all my adventures as a Knight of the Prince, this was my most terrifying. My true fight was within me—*fear*. With death staring me in the face, would my faith in the Prince give me the courage I needed to stand firm?

One of the Shadow Warriors drew his sword, anxious to taste first blood. Two of them moved closer to us.

"Swear your allegiance and bow before me or die!" The words shot like poisoned darts. I slowly began to realize just how truly evil Histen was.

William spoke first. "Our allegiance is to the Prince and His Father, the true King of Arrethtrae!"

Though they were monstrous men, all four of them winced when William spoke of the Prince. Even His name was powerful!

The Shadow Warrior closest to William struck him on the brow with the hilt of his sword. William fell to his knees and covered his head with his hands. Blood spilled between his fingers and onto the ground.

Before I could kneel and help him, Histen stepped forward and gripped my neck with his left hand. It was then that I remembered the Prince's Silent Warriors.

"The King reigns—and His Son!" I voiced what I could through Histen's tightening grip.

Histen and the four Shadow Warriors bellowed in wicked laughter.

"The Silent Warriors will not save you, knave! I own this kingdom now. The former King and His weak Son are finished here." As Histen spoke, his heinous smile turned to a sneer of disgust. "I have finished them in Arrethtrae, and I will return one day to His own kingdom and kill them both!"

My fear, though I know not why, instantly left me. I knew I could stand and die with honor. Though Histen tried to demean the King and the Prince, his voice betrayed him, and I knew that Histen feared the Prince more than any fear I would ever feel for Histen.

"You are not the true king of Arrethtrae," I said. "You have betrayed the people and lied to them. You care only for power and control. You are not who the people think you are…I see what a truly evil leader you are."

Histen glared at me with eyes that spewed hatred like poison from a viper. His hand tightened around my neck, nearly closing off my air. I felt the rocks in the wall behind me press into my head and back.

He leaned into my face. His handsome features were twisted into a gut-wrenching evil countenance. My vision started to blur, and my mind was beginning to fade. In my waning, I saw a vision of the Prince standing on the roof of the building across the alleyway.

Death must not be far away, I thought.

"You are right about one thing, peasant," Histen said in a deep guttural voice that was nearly a whisper. "I am not who the people think I am." I knew he wanted to kill me. Hate seemed to completely possess him. "I…" His grip tightened. "Am…" Tighter…I could not breathe now. "…Lucius!"

His right hand revealed a dagger that would soon spill my blood. He pulled back to strike. From the corner of my eye, I saw one of the Shadow Warriors raise his sword to slay William, who was still facedown on the ground.

This is the end, I thought. I was to die at the hands of Lucius—the evil enemy of the Prince. In my final moments, the vision of the Prince seemed so real. His sword was drawn, and He beckoned me to…to…fight?

The dagger started its deadly plunge toward my chest. Time nearly froze.

I could not fail the Prince and die such a feeble death. He had trained me for this very fight—a fight against the evil one.

The dagger flashed closer.

Maybe I would die, but only after exhausting every fiber of strength and will in my body.

Yes, my Prince, I will fight…fight for You!

The dagger was nearing its target—my heart. With all my strength and speed, I swept my left forearm across my chest to deflect the dagger, now only inches from my chest, and simultaneously turned my body. It was just enough— the dagger skinned my left shoulder and struck the rocks behind me.

My body was turned slightly to the left, and my right hand found the hilt of my sword in an instant. I heard Lucius curse and recoil for another strike, but I beat him to it. My left hand joined my right at my sword as I partially withdrew it from the scabbard with great force. My fisted hands and the hilt of my sword struck Lucius's stomach. His suffocating grip on my neck was immediately broken as he doubled over from the blow.

"Move, William!" I shouted as I saw the blade of the Shadow Warrior descend on him. William rolled with the speed of a panther. The sword missed him and hit the ground with tremendous force. A shower of sparks flew in all directions.

There was a moment of chaos that allowed me to spring toward William. My sword was now fully drawn, and I lunged at the Shadow Warrior who was making another strike as William tried to scramble to his feet. My sword found its mark, and the Shadow Warrior collapsed in an instant.

Lucius tried to give orders, but the air had left his lungs; he could only gesture toward us.

William was now on his feet with his sword drawn. We were side by side and ready to fight, though I knew this fight would be our last. The three remaining Shadow Warriors advanced quickly—then hesitated, looking past us at something approaching from behind. I did not dare turn around and see what it was.

"Good afternoon, gentlemen," came Rob's familiar voice from my right. "It looks like you are in need of some assistance."

Rob joined to my right and Barrett to William's left.

"We will fight for the Prince and for our brothers," Barrett said.

Our brief moment of relief quickly transformed into the seriousness of battle with our brothers in arms. Rob and Barrett joined us either to save us or to die with us. There was no worse enemy than this, and we all knew it.

"Kill them!" Lucius shouted.

We took our stance and prepared for the onslaught, but they still held back.

"They were trained by the Prince," one of the Shadow Warriors said over his shoulder. He did not take his eyes off of us.

Lucius moved forward with his sword drawn. "Attack or I will kill you myself!" he yelled to his men as he lunged toward me.

The Shadow Warriors followed…each one to one of us.

The battle began.

The rage on Lucius's face matched the fury of his sword. It was a duel to the death, and I knew I must rely on the Prince's training. Lucius was quick and cunning. Our swords met in a ferocious volley of thrusts, cuts, and slices.

The Prince had prepared me for this battle. I saw Him in every motion of my sword. My muscles had memorized the moves, and my sword seemed to know exactly what to do. I felt the Prince in my arms and hands. I gave control to Him. My sword flew to match each cut and thrust of this beast. The sword of the Prince would protect me…deliver me. My confidence during the battle was surreal; all fear was gone. I had been trained by the Master Himself—the Master of the Sword!

The close quarters of the alleyway forced the four separate sword fights to spread out. The clashing swords echoed off the walls, which added to the intensity of the battle. I saw Rob take a cut across his shoulder, but it was not deep. He, William, and Barrett fought like the valiant warriors they were trained to be. The Shadow Warriors were huge, but we were fast and knew their tricks. The battle raged on.

Lucius thrust. I parried and countered, but he caught my cut with the flat of his sword. He quickly countered with a cut across my chest. *Whoosh!* I leaped back to miss his blade and lost my balance. I fell to my knees. Lucius pounced toward me with a vertical cut that I caught with my sword just above my head. I threw my left leg in a circular motion to trip him, and his legs flew out from under him. I seized the opportunity to scramble to my feet. Lucius recovered quickly, and we engaged our swords again.

I saw William counter a cut with a quick thrust that found its mark. The Shadow Warrior dropped his sword and clutched his chest as he fell to the ground.

William was closest to Barrett and joined him against his foe.

The fight quickly turned in our favor, and I saw the exasperation on Lucius's face grow more vivid with each passing moment. He backed off quickly as Barrett's opponent fell from a fatal wound. The last Shadow Warrior turned and ran up the alley. Lucius quickly mounted his stallion and galloped away.

"I will be back to kill all of you!" he screamed.

"Praise to the King and His Son, the Prince!" we shouted in return.

The battle was over; the Knights of the Prince had pre-vailed. We breathed a temporary sigh of relief.

"Thank you, gentlemen," I said to Rob and Barrett. "You came not a moment too soon."

"I was worried when you didn't show at Barrett's, so we decided to come for you," Rob said as Barrett bandaged his arm.

"And I'm glad you did," William said.

He looked a mess because of the blood from his initial head wound. The bleeding had nearly stopped, and I washed the cut with clean water.

"I don't know about you, gentlemen, but I'm ready to go home," I said.

The rush of the fight was leaving my body. I was tired…bone tired.

On our journey back south, we moved carefully, avoiding all possible contact with people.

I thought about the dark shadow that now hung over Arrethtrae. Lucius's power was going to grow with each passing day. These were becoming dark days indeed.

My Prince, when will You return? I thought…I yearned.

CHAPTER FIFTEEN

TAKEN!

 "Awake, Cedric!"

The words sounded hollow and distant. I tried to understand them, but my mind refused. I had found that place in sleep so deep and peaceful that one would rather have a roof fall on him than awaken. I sensed a tugging on my arm and fought to gain consciousness, but my recovery was slow.

"It is time. We must go immediately. Wake up!"

My eyes focused on the massive frame bent over me. "Keef, is that you?" I asked groggily.

"Yes, my old friend," Keef said. "The time has come to go home. Rise up and come with me. We are all going home!"

I thought I saw him return an object to his pouch.

My limbs felt as heavy as lead, but I managed to grab his arm, and he swung me to my feet.

"It is very good to see you, Keef." I smiled and wiped away the sleep. "What is happening?"

"It is the King. He has called us all home to His kingdom. The Silent Warriors are spread throughout the land
and are gathering the Knights of the Prince this very
moment. Ships are waiting for us. We must move everyone
quickly and quietly before the Dark Knight discovers us."

I wondered how Keef and the other Silent Warriors
would be able to orchestrate such a rescue and exodus quietly
and smoothly.

"Hurry, Cedric," Keef said. "We must move quickly. Do
not take anything except your sword. Move toward the
ships at the docks. You must not speak to anyone until you
reach the ships."

"Why not?" I asked. "Shouldn't I help you gather the
knights?"

"That is not possible. You see, not everyone who claims
to be for the Prince will be taken. The Silent Warriors have
been watching everyone claiming to be a Knight of the
Prince, and we know those who are truly His followers."

Keef read my concern as I thought of all the people I
had labored to reach for the Prince. Who would be missing
when I got to the ships?

"I'm sorry, Cedric," Keef said. "I must leave now and
gather more of the knights. I will see you across the sea, my
friend. Take care and do not waste any time. The Prince
awaits you!"

"Farewell, Keef," I said as we exited my home.

He turned north, and I turned south toward the docks.
Please, let all my close brothers be there.

I walked a few paces and turned back to ask Keef a
final question, but he was already gone. Did he say the

Prince awaits, or was my mind still foggy with sleep?

There was a silent exodus of people out of the city. Men, women, and children sprinkled the streets and alleyways—all heading south to the docks. As I moved, I couldn't help but increase my speed with each step.

Would the Prince be waiting at the ships, or must I wait until after the voyage to see my friend, my teacher, my Lord?

I recognized most of the people silently making their way to the ships and smiled a salutation.

I stopped to help carry a little boy belonging to a family with six children. The mother and father's arms were already full of smaller sleeping children. It slowed my pace, but I did not care. We were all going home!

I wondered how we could possibly get everyone out of the city without being discovered. Surely someone would awaken and reveal our flight.

As these thoughts occupied my mind, I nearly tripped over a motionless body on the side of the street. I stopped to help, thinking this person was one of our own and was hurt. As I bent closer to the body, I realized it was a man sleeping so heavily that he nearly seemed dead.

I later learned that the Silent Warriors had tainted all drinking water with a sleeping compound. The entire kingdom was asleep and would stay that way for many hours. Even we were affected, but the Silent Warriors possessed a counter agent to awaken us.

The little boy I was carrying was now fully awake and asked to walk on his own. I set him by his father's side. He smiled in gratitude, and I moved on at my previous quickened pace.

As I approached the docks, I saw two ships already underway out to sea. They were full of fellow knights. The silent mass of people flowed steadily from the streets and onto the ships, all of them passing by one man—*the Prince!*

I could not contain my enthusiasm. My quickened pace turned to a full run.

No longer was He wearing the clothes of a peasant. He was now clothed in full royal attire, which framed His majestic character. His magnificent sword hung near His side. The sight of Him demanded awe and respect. This was only a glimpse of what He had given up to set us free. Soon I would see the splendor of His kingdom and all its riches. He did this for me!

My mind could hardly grasp that statement as truth. The King and His Son must love us more than we thought possible—more than we could love even our own children. What a strange way to save the kingdom!

The Prince looked at me as I came to Him. Those same penetrating eyes smiled at me. Tears spilled onto my cheeks as I knelt before Him and took in His loving gaze. Just as He once before had lowered Himself for me as a peasant, He knelt to one knee and put His hand behind my neck.

His voice was quiet and sincere. "Well done, Cedric. Well done!"

I lowered my head and wept. Oh, how I had craved to hear those words. They were the prize for all my journeys…all my struggles. I cherish them to this day more than gold.

The Prince raised me to my feet and hugged me as though I was His son. I was already home!

THE GREAT BATTLE

 Our arrival in the kingdom across the sea was glorious. William and I shared our stories with many fellow knights, and the Silent Warriors captivated us with all they had seen and experienced as well.

One particularly joyful reunion was with my old friend Leinad. He had devoted his entire life to loyal service of the King. I listened to all his grand adventures as a gallant knight once again, but this time I was spellbound because those stories were so significant to the arrival of the Prince.

After the great reunion and celebration, we resumed our training under the Prince once again. He was preparing us—preparing us for this very day, this very battle.

NOW YOU KNOW MY STORY. I was but a peasant, hungry and clothed in rags. Today I share the line of gallant Knights of the Prince. I wear the armor of the Prince and will fight beside Him this hour. This is where you found me, and this is where I must leave you…at the kingdom's edge. This is the battle to regain Arrethtrae. Never in the history of man was there ever a battle between such powerful forces, nor will there ever be again.

The Dark Knight must be conquered!

After our departure from Arrethtrae, the Dark Knight used our mysterious disappearance to further frighten the people and secure his control over the entire kingdom. He was in his own perverted glory for a time. Fear ruled the people. If they did not serve him, they were eliminated. But now his time has come. The Prince will make sure of that.

There is the Prince now—His white stallion beneath and His magnificent sword before! Nothing can stand before the Prince. He is truly invincible.

The sound of a mighty and evil force approaches, but I am not afraid. I am on the side of the Prince.

On whose side are you?

DISCUSSION QUESTIONS

To further facilitate the understanding of the biblical allegory of this series, a few discussion questions and answers are provided below.

CHAPTER 1

1. We hear about a procession of Noble Knights. Who do they represent biblically?

2. Cedric tells us that the Noble Knights handed out scraps of food to people to show their superiority over them. Cedric says, "I believe they did it to inflate their egos." Find the parable in the Bible about a Pharisee and a tax collector praying in a synagogue. Also look up Matthew 6:5–7. How do you think God feels about public displays of religiosity?

3. Leinad mentions the "Sword of the King," but it is kept in his trunk in the corner. What do you think this represents?

4. Cedric meets a "man from a distant land." Who do you think this man is? Who does he represent?

CHAPTER 2

1. Who does the Dark Knight represent?

2. After the Noble Knights finish their training in the city square, a shop owner demands justice after a girl steals bread from his store. The most prestigious Noble Knight, Kifus, begins to execute judgment according to the Code, meaning that

the girl will lose her right hand. But the mysterious stranger Cedric met in the previous chapter duels with Kifus to save the girl. This event represents what other biblical event? Find the passage and read it.

3. Cedric cannot remember if the sword the stranger carries is Leinad's "Sword of the King." And when the stranger reveals that He is the King's Son, the Noble Knights do not recognize Him. They had stopped listening to Leinad's message that a deliverer was coming. This represents when Jesus revealed that He was God's Son, but the Pharisees refused to believe Him. They weren't familiar enough with the prophecies of His coming as found in the Word of God, spoken by the prophets. Why is it important for us to study God's Word?

4. The King's Son rebukes the Noble Knights three times in this chapter. What do these exchanges represent?

5. Who do you think Cedric represents? Why? Find a passage in the Bible that supports your conclusion.

6. Cedric reflects, "In my heart I knew I must answer one question, *Do I really believe that this man is the Son of the King?*" Just as Cedric was required to answer this question about the Prince, so must we decide whether or not to believe that Jesus is really the Son of God. Once this decision is made, what must follow?

DISCUSSION QUESTIONS

CHAPTER 3

1. At the beginning of the chapter, Cedric reflects, "I have learned that the hardest, most difficult times of my life caused the most growth in my character" (read 1 Peter 1:6–7). Have you found this to be true for you as well?

2. The Prince uses His sword to train Cedric and the other Knights of the Prince. What does this symbolize?

3. Cedric narrates, "Dark shadows usually hide dark deeds." What do you think about this? Find passages in the Bible regarding light and darkness.

4. The Prince tells Cedric and William that one day He must return to His Father's kingdom (read John 13:36–37). However, the Prince also says He will return for those faithful to the King and bring them to His kingdom for their final training. Then together they will completely destroy the Dark Knight. This represents the biblical prophecies concerning Jesus' second coming. Can you find some of those prophecies?

5. Who do the Silent Warriors represent?

6. The Prince tells Cedric and William that the Dark Knight and his Shadow Warriors are coming to attack the kingdom because they want revenge on the King for defeating them in battle. What does the foreshadowing of the coming struggle with the Dark Knight represent?

CHAPTER 4

1. In this chapter, Cedric and William encounter a Shadow Warrior who is about to kill a man. They

attempt to save the shop owner, but they are unable to defeat the Shadow Warrior. When they are about to be overcome, the Prince arrives and sends the Shadow Warrior running for his life. What two biblical events does this event portray?

2. After battling against the Shadow Warrior for some time, Cedric sees William use a combination taught by the Prince. Cedric realizes that he had been relying on his own skill and not on the training he received from the Prince. What might this mean for you personally? How does God empower you to overcome sin in your life?

3. The only reason Cedric and William were able to remain alive during their battle with the Shadow Warrior was because there were two of them. Jesus knew about the importance of having a partner with you when you enter into missions. Find a verse that supports why you think this is true.

CHAPTER 5

1. At the beginning of this chapter, the Prince begins to train His Knights with the use of the shield. What does this represent? Find a passage of Scripture to support you.

2. The focus of this chapter is an attack on the Prince by three Noble Knights. What does this event portray?

3. Who does Kifus represent?

4. As the three Noble Knights are leaving, one turns and asks the Prince, "Are you truly the King's Son?" Who do you think this Knight may have represented?

DISCUSSION QUESTIONS

CHAPTER 6

1. In this chapter the Prince cries a single tear for the people of Chessington; we see how much the Prince loves the people. He also loves children, and He tells them a story as they surround Him and sit on His lap. What biblical event does this portray?

2. The Prince is so moved when He sees the people of Chessington starving that He sends His Knights to feed them with food sent from His Father's kingdom. What biblical event does this portray?

3. Article 3 of the Code states, "Offer compassion to the weak, the destitute, the widowed, and the poor" (*Kingdom's Hope*). The Noble Knights' idea of compassion had become twisted with the passing of time, so the Prince teaches His Knights about the nature of true compassion. This is something Jesus also emphasized during His ministry on earth. Compassion is more than just feeling something; it's doing something. Have you ever acted on compassion for someone? How did that make you feel? Has someone ever been compassionate to you? How did that make you feel?

CHAPTER 7

1. There are three direct allusions to Scripture in this chapter. What are those three events, and where are they in the Bible?

2. As the Prince surrenders to Kifus and the Noble Knights, He throws His sword deep into the forest. What does this symbolize?

3. The Prince had the power to save Himself, but instead He gave Himself up to save His knights. When Jesus was taken in the Garden of

Gethsemane, He had the power to free himself and to even destroy His enemies if He so desired, but His mission was so much greater than self-preservation and revenge. He restrained Himself from acting manlike and sacrificed Himself to save us from our sins, thus acting godlike. How do you act when you are persecuted for being a Christian? Can you find a verse that tells us how we are supposed to act?

CHAPTER 8

1. In this chapter it appears as though the Dark Knight is victorious over the Prince by having Him killed. This is clearly symbolic of Jesus Christ's death on the cross. What is the irony regarding those responsible for His death and their reason for killing Him?

CHAPTER 9

1. Cedric and some of the Knights of the Prince are hiding in Barrett's shop after the Prince dies. Find verses in the Bible that show what this represents.

2. The resurrection of Christ is depicted in this chapter when the Prince appears to Cedric and a few of the other knights. Why is the Resurrection such an important part of the gospel?

3. Cedric and the other knights were afraid after the Prince was killed. What gave them courage to take up the mission the Prince had given them? What gives you courage to stand up for Jesus?

CHAPTER 10

1. Cedric and William embark on a mission to another city to recruit followers of the Prince. Here

they are challenged by a group of men that nearly kills them. In a moment of peril Cedric cries, "The King reigns—and His Son!" Who comes to their aid? Can you find a Bible passage where a disciple receives help from an angel of God?

2. Can you think of a time in your life when you knew that God intervened to help you out of a difficult situation?

CHAPTER 11

1. Keef, a Silent Warrior, tells Cedric a story about the Dark Knight and his rebellion against the King. What does this story represent biblically, and where do you find it in Scripture?

2. Keef tells Cedric another story about the great sword fight between the Prince and Lucius. What does this represent, and why is the symbolism of the sword important in this scene? Find Scripture to back up your answer.

3. The Bible tells us in 1 Corinthians 10:13, "No temptation has overtaken you except such as is common to man; but God is faithful, who will not allow you to be tempted beyond what you are able, but with the temptation will also make the way of escape, that you may be able to bear it." God promises to provide a way out of every temptation we face. Using this verse and the example of Jesus, what should we do to overcome temptation?

CHAPTER 12

1. In this chapter, Cedric and William find themselves caught up in a battle between Silent

Warriors and Shadow Warriors. What do they learn from the Silent Warriors, and how does this apply to us today?

2. What are you doing to ensure that you are prepared when Jesus returns?

CHAPTER 13

1. Cedric, William, and Rob help a man bitten by a snake and then tell him about the Prince. This story changes the man's heart. What does this represent, and what Bible verse talks about such a transformation in a person?

2. Jesus has called all of His believers to share the Good News of salvation with others. Sometimes this takes courage and boldness. Have you ever been given the opportunity to share the transforming story of Jesus with anyone? What did you do? God will provide the opportunity and the courage if you ask Him.

CHAPTER 14

1. In this chapter, Cedric and his friends come face-to-face with the Dark Knight and his Shadow Warriors. Cedric finally realizes that he should not give up, but fight with the sword that the Prince gave him. What Bible verse tells us how to fight the devil?

CHAPTER 15

1. At the end of the book, the Knights of the Prince are all secretly taken out of the kingdom. What does this represent, and what Scripture passages back up your answer?

2. Cedric meets the Prince at the docks and kneels before Him. He craves to hear the words "Well done!" These are the same words Jesus uses in a parable to explain the kingdom of heaven. Find that parable and the words Jesus spoke.

3. Later, in the Epilogue, Cedric arrives in the kingdom across the sea. What do you think this represents?

4. Jesus said in Matthew 7:14, "Narrow is the gate and difficult is the way which leads to life, and there are few who find it." The Bible teaches that there is only one way to heaven, and that is through believing on Jesus Christ. In Romans, there are seven verses that explain what and why we must believe in order to be saved. These verses are listed at the end of the answers to the discussion questions. Would you like to ask Jesus to come into your life and save you for all eternity?

ANSWERS TO
DISCUSSION QUESTIONS

1. The Pharisees.

2. Luke 18:9–14. Jesus clearly states that public displays of piety are hypocritical. This is also explained in Luke 11:42–43.

3. The sword represents the Word of God, so this represents the four hundred years of God's silence between the prophecies of Malachi and the coming of John the Baptist.

4. This man is the Prince, the son of the King; He represents Jesus Christ. The reference to His eyes, which "burned like fire" is a foreshadowing of His second coming (see Revelation 19:11–16).

CHAPTER 2

1. The Dark Knight represents Satan.

2. John 8:1–11. This event also represents the transition from the age of the law to the age of grace. Jesus' reaction to the woman caught in adultery is indicative of this shift.

3. The Bible says in 2 Timothy 2:15, "Be diligent to present yourself approved to God, a worker who does not need to be ashamed, rightly dividing the word of truth." Find more verses that address our need to read and study God's Word.

4. Jesus calling the Pharisees hypocrites (see Matthew 23:13–29).

5. In this specific instance, Cedric represents all of the disciples of Jesus. The Prince asks Cedric to be a Knight of the Prince, just like Jesus asks the disciples to be fishers of men (Matthew 4:18–22; Mark 1:16–18). In a broader sense, Cedric symbolizes all followers of Christ, including you.

6. Cedric chose to believe in the Prince and then followed Him. That is what God requires of us as well. Jesus said in Mark 10:21, "Then Jesus, looking at him, loved him, and said to him, 'One thing you lack: Go your way, sell whatever you have and give to the poor, and you will have treasure in heaven; and come, take up the cross, and follow Me.'"

CHAPTER 3

1. Answer based on personal experience.

2. Jesus teaching the disciples using parables, Old Testament Scripture, and Himself, since Jesus is the Word in the flesh (John 1:1–3).

3. One example is John 3:19–20.

4. Revelation 19:11–16; 1 Thessalonians 4:16–18.

5. Angels.

6. This represents the prophecies of the coming antichrist and his rule on earth.

CHAPTER 4

1. This event first portrays when the disciples fail to cast out a demon but Jesus succeeds (Matthew 17:14–21). The second biblical event is when the demons recognize Jesus and beg not to be destroyed (Matthew 8:28–29).

2. Pray; read, memorize, and quote Scripture; sing praises to God.

3. Mark 6:7; Ecclesiastes 4:9.

CHAPTER 5

1. The armor of God as described in Ephesians 6:10–18.

2. This event portrays the times when the Pharisees tried to trap Jesus into violating the Law. One instance is recorded in Matthew 22:15–22.

3. Caiaphas, the head Pharisee (Matthew 26:3).

4. Nicodemus (John 3:1–21).

CHAPTER 6

1. When Jesus lays hands on and blesses children in Mark 10:13–16.

2. This event has dual meaning. First, this event directly parallels the feeding of the five thousand as told in Matthew 14:14–21. This event also symbolizes Jesus feeding them spiritually by giving them the truth of salvation (Matthew 4:4.)

3. Answer based on personal experience.

CHAPTER 7

1. (1) The Last Supper (Luke 22:19–23); (2) the Garden of Gethsemane (Luke 22:39–46); (3) the disciples fleeing (Matthew 26:56).

2. Jesus' silence during His trials (Mark 15:3–5).

3. Answer based on personal experience (Matthew 5:44).

ANSWERS TO DISCUSSION QUESTIONS

CHAPTER 8

1. The irony is that the Pharisees (the Noble Knights) were responsible for killing Jesus (the Prince), God the Father's Son (the King's Son), and yet they thought they were serving the Father because they believed Jesus was committing blasphemy by claiming to be the Father's Son. In their pride and ignorance, the Pharisees had become a tool of Satan (the Dark Knight).

CHAPTER 9

1. In John 20:19 the Bible says that the disciples were in a room with the doors shut for fear of the Jews.

2. It shows God's supreme power by overcoming even death.

3. Seeing the Prince overcome death and understanding that everything He said was true.

CHAPTER 10

1. Two Silent Warriors come to their aid. Peter is freed and led out of prison by an angel in Acts 12:5–12. Also, Paul and Silas receive help when an earthquake opens the jail doors and their chains fall off (Acts 16:26).

2. Answer based on personal experience.

CHAPTER 11

1. This represents when Satan rebelled against God in heaven and convinced a third of the angels to follow him. Michael and the holy angels overcame Lucifer and the demons, and they were cast out of heaven. This is found in Isaiah 14:12–17 and Revelation 12:3–12.

2. This represents when Satan tempted Jesus in the wilderness (Matthew 4:1–11). The symbolism of the sword is important in that there was a tremendous spiritual sword fight between Jesus and Satan. Satan quoted Scripture erroneously to try to tempt Jesus, but Jesus quoted the true Word of God to defeat Satan in all of the three temptations. The Bible tells us in Ephesians 6:17 that the only offensive weapon we have against the devil is the Word of God.

3. Look for the way out that God has provided, and quote Scripture to defeat the devil, just as Jesus did.

CHAPTER 12

1. They learn that something significant is about to happen and that they should all be ready. Jesus warns us to be ready through a parable found in Matthew 25:1–13.

2. Answer based on personal experience.

CHAPTER 13

1. This represents sharing the gospel of Jesus Christ with a nonbeliever. Second Corinthians 5:17 says "Therefore, if anyone is in Christ, he is a new creation; old things have passed away; behold, all things have become new."

2. Answer based on personal experience.

CHAPTER 14

1. James 4:7–8: "Therefore submit to God. Resist the devil and he will flee from you. Draw near to God and He will draw near to you."

CHAPTER 15

1. This is the rapture of the Church as described in Matthew 24:39–41; 1 Corinthians 15:52; and 1 Thessalonians 4:16–18.

2. Matthew 25:21: "His lord said to him, 'Well done, good and faithful servant; you were faithful over a few things, I will make you ruler over many things. Enter into the joy of your lord.'"

3. The saints' arrival in heaven.

4. The following Bible verses explain what a person must understand and believe to be saved:

· Romans 3:10—"As it is written: 'There is none righteous, no, not one.'"

· Romans 3:23—"For all have sinned and fall short of the glory of God."

· Romans 5:12—"Therefore, just as through one man sin entered the world, and death through sin, and thus death spread to all men, because all sinned."

· Romans 5:8—"But God demonstrates His own love toward us, in that while we were still sinners, Christ died for us."

· Romans 6:23—"For the wages of sin is death, but the gift of God is eternal life in Christ Jesus our Lord."

· Romans 10:13—"Whoever calls on the name of the LORD shall be saved."

· Romans 10:9—"If you confess with your mouth the Lord Jesus and believe in your heart that God has raised Him from the dead, you will be saved."

Deliverance
Written for Kingdom's Edge

Music by Emily Elizabeth Black
Lyrics by Chuck Black
Edited by Brittney Dyanne Black

Tenderly

mp

Oo- Ah-

Come see the man from a dis-tant land. Come hear his words of hope. He speaks of a

king-dom of the heart, call-ing all to be a part.

Oo- Ah- Come see the man from a dis-tant land.

Cham- pion of poor and meek. His words of truth no-ble men des-pise. See how now he

AUTHOR'S COMMENTARY

This story about Cedric and his life-changing encounter with the Prince from a distant land can be read simply for its adventure, but it was written with a purpose of greater significance: to spark the interest of readers of all ages in the greatest story ever told. No writer can create a saga more profound or more fascinating than the true story of Jesus Christ and His redeeming visit to earth. The full impact of the Gospels does not completely grip us until we attain significant spiritual maturity. Thus, as Jesus so often taught in parables to awaken our minds to the deeper truths of His kingdom, I have attempted to help you take a fresh look at a story that has transformed lives for twenty centuries and circled the globe thousands of times.

The power of a parable is dramatic. The words you've just read are original, but the story is not. Nearly every scene in the book represents a specific event that took place two thousand years ago. This story can be read for simple enjoyment or for the deeper spiritual analogies of the single most significant event in human history. Please read on if you are curious about understanding these analogies.

The story is obviously focused on Jesus Christ, the Prince, and His three-year ministry, His sacrifice, and His resurrection. Jesus' followers have always found it difficult to grasp the reality of warfare in the spirit world. However, that warfare is as real as the sword fights that occurred during the Middle Ages, and this story attempts to bring that spiritual warfare into a more comprehensible physical world.

The Bible teaches that our only offensive weapon against Satan and his demons is the Word of God (Ephesians 6:17). The climactic duel of the universe occurred when Satan tempted Jesus in the wilderness. The fate of all mankind was on His shoulders. Jesus was victorious because He used Scripture, His sword, in each temptation (Matthew 4:1–11). It is a perfect example for us to follow, but we must have a sword, and the sword must be sharpened and polished as Cedric did in preparation for his battles. The sword is therefore a point of primary focus throughout the story.

Hebrews 4:12 states:

For the word of God is living and powerful, and sharper than any two-edged sword, piercing even to the division of soul and spirit, and of joints and marrow, and is a discerner of the thoughts and intents of the heart.

The sword represents the Word of God, but *only* the Word of God. The Pharisees had God's Word also, but Jesus was fiercely disappointed with them. What they lacked was the true meaning or the intent of God's Word. Thus, the Code represents the true meaning of God's Word. The Noble Knights, representing the Pharisees, used their swords to esteem themselves and therefore failed the King and the people. The sword is used to defeat evil but also to show compassion and love to the humble and weak. God's Word should be written on our hearts and should not be just a set of rules to be followed.

Cedric represents all men, women, and children who have trusted in Jesus Christ as Lord and Savior. He spans the age from Peter to the last person called before we are taken home. I hope you will see yourself as Cedric, whom the Prince chose to elevate from spiritual poverty to heir of His heavenly kingdom. Cedric is an unlikely knight because he is poor and untrained, just as we are unlikely candidates to be children of God because of our sinful natures. It is only through the love, power, and sacrifice of Jesus that we are made worthy.

Other personifications include Kifus, who represents Caiaphas, the high priest (Matthew 26:57). The Silent Warriors are God's holy angels, and the Shadow Warriors are Satan's demons. The Dark Knight, Lucius, represents Lucifer and the beast of the end times. Leinad represents the prophets who brought God's Word to the people.

Some scene analogies include the temptation of Christ, the miraculous feeding of the hungry, Jesus' love for children, the casting out of demons, the Crucifixion, the Resurrection, and the Rapture. There are more analogies throughout the story. In fact, nearly every word, scene, and name was written with symbolism and analogy in mind. The discussion questions were written to provide further insight into the symbolism of the story.

The final battle that is about to take place as the story begins and ends is the ultimate battle between good and evil. Jesus will defeat Satan and his demons once and for all. If you have trusted Jesus as your Lord and Savior, you are a child of God—a saint. As the saints of God, we will be part of that victorious army. In the interim, let us put on the whole armor of God and wage war of eternal significance as soldiers for our Lord and Savior, Jesus Christ.

> Finally, my brethren, be strong in the Lord and in the power of His might. Put on the whole armor of God, that you may be able to stand against the wiles of the devil. (Ephesians 6:10–11)

It is my most earnest desire to bring honor and glory to God through this story of a Prince from a distant land. May your zeal for God's Word be renewed, and may you also be worthy of those welcoming words spoken by Jesus: "Well done, good and faithful servant.... Enter into the joy of your lord" (Matthew 25:21).

Discover the ultimate battle between good and evil

If You Love the Kingdom Series
—You'll Love the Knights of Arrethtrae

Powerful Allegories, Biblical Values

Sir Kendrick and the Castle of Bel Lione
In this first of Chuck Black's companion series to the popular Kingdom series, Sir Kendrick and Sir Duncan are sent to stop a dangerous new order that threatens their mission to serve the King.

Sir Bentley and Holbrook Court
In this second installment in Chuck Black's Knights of Arrethtrae series, readers will be drawn to the action, adventure, and romance of the story of Sir Bentley, an honorable young knight who battles the forces of evil and discovers the power of compassion to overcome the destructiveness of greed.

Sir Dalton and the Shadow Heart
Sir Dalton, a knight in training, is young, well-liked, and a natural leader. He has earned the respect and admiration of his fellow knights, and especially the beautiful Lady Brynn. But to defend the kingdom, Dalton must face the evil Shadow Warrior—this time will he survive?

Lady Carliss and the Waters of Moorue
Determined, smart and a master of both the sword and the bow, Lady Carliss races against time to save Sir Dalton's life, but an evil plot foils her efforts and she must choose between saving him and saving countless others.